PUSHKIN P
In associatior
WALTER PRE

THE GHOST OF FRÉDÉRIC CHOPIN

In a world where we have so much choice, curation is becoming increasingly key. Walter Presents was first set up to champion brilliant drama from around the world and bring it to a wider audience.

Now, in collaboration with Pushkin Press, we're hoping to do the same thing for foreign literature: translating brilliant books into English, introducing them to readers who are hungry for quality fiction.

The title of this book immediately caught my eye. Set in post-Communist Prague, the story revolves around a journalist who is tasked with investigating a seemingly ordinary widow, with no previous musical training, who claims she is visited by the ghost of Frédéric Chopin. What's more, the great maestro is dictating dozens of wonderful musical compositions to her. Is it a hoax, a con or has the virtuoso's spirit really taken hold of her? Roll over Beethoven, here comes *The Ghost of Frédéric Chopin*, a finely crafted, delicious, spellbinding mystery.

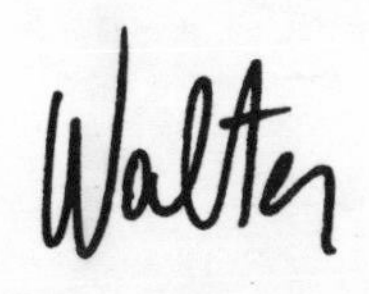

THE GHOST OF FRÉDÉRIC CHOPIN

ÉRIC
FAYE

TRANSLATED FROM THE FRENCH
BY SAM TAYLOR

PUSHKIN PRESS
In association with
WALTER PRESENTS

Pushkin Press
71–75 Shelton Street
London WC2H 9JQ

The Ghost of Frédéric Chopin was first published as
La télégraphiste de Chopin by Éditions du Seuil in Paris, 2019

First published by Pushkin Press in 2021

1 3 5 7 9 8 6 4 2

ISBN 13: 978-1-78227-722-4

Epigraph from *Forbidden Colours* by Yukio Mishima,
trans. Alfred H. Marks (Penguin, 2008)

Designed and typeset by Tetragon, London
Printed and bound by CPI Group (UK) Ltd, Croydon, CR0 4YY

www.pushkinpress.com

This novel is very loosely inspired
by the life of Rosemary Brown
(1916–2001)

In artistic works, there is a twofold possibility of existence, he believed. Just as an ancient lotus seed will flower again when dug up and replanted, the work of art that is said to possess everlasting life can live again in the hearts of all times, all countries.

YUKIO MISHIMA

PART ONE

I

THE COBBLESTONES were damp and slippery but, all things considered, he decided it was better to risk twisting his ankle than to lose sight of the woman walking quickly a hundred feet ahead of him; this woman who, according to Slaný, was in communication with Frédéric Chopin a century and a half after his death. A strange case… If anyone had told him, ten years before, that ten years later – on this gloomy Monday, an All Saints' Day in the twilight of the century – he would no longer be a member of the secret police but would be reduced to playing private detective in a country that had been sliced in half and converted to capitalism, he would have cursed the future. Then again, if that same someone had added that he would be spying on a former school dinner lady who transcribed dozens of posthumous scores dictated to her by the Polish composer, the fanciful part of his personality would have been awakened and he would have thought that, on further consideration, the future merited a closer look. And if, moreover, that mysterious someone had told him that the woman in question was the widow of a recalcitrant individual whom he had followed years before, he would have seen in his future occupation of detective the suggestive glow of destiny, of a torch handed on from past to present.

Yes, this woman and her ghost made a change from those dissidents who haunted bars into the small hours under the previous regime, those damned dissidents who had given him so many nagging chest infections over the years, from sitting and waiting in unheated cars, because this StB agent had suffered from weak lungs ever since he was a little boy.

The woman he was following, whose fame was starting to spread far beyond the mountains of Bohemia, had been called Věra Foltýnova since her marriage, twenty-six years earlier. She was born Věra Kowalski one June day in 1938 – nobody remembered the exact date – which made her fifty-seven on that particular All Saints' Day in 1995.

When she reappeared in his field of vision, the former StB agent breathed a sigh of relief. It wasn't the first time she'd briefly vanished from sight that day, since leaving her apartment; each time he lost her like that, he started sweating, despite all his experience of shadowing people from a distance. And then her chubby figure would materialize again, a mischievous smile on her face. If that was the game, he was happy to play along.

She had been constantly on the move since mid-morning. And the detective hadn't had a chance to rest in the past week.

Now that the street had straightened out, he thought things might get easier. He would follow her more closely to make sure he didn't lose her again. Where could she be headed? One thing was sure: she wasn't going home, because her home was in the opposite direction. It was almost noon… When she went into a food shop, he exhaled and celebrated this brief respite by lighting a cigarette. Just then, he remembered that the journalist had asked him to get in touch as soon as he had some news. He spotted a telephone booth a dozen feet from where he stood. It rang twice before the journalist answered.

'Ludvík Slaný, Česká televize.'

'It's Pavel Černý. You asked me to keep you in the loop, and I've got a moment now because she's nipped into a shop. She left home just before ten and went to Olšany to put flowers on her husband's grave. Right now, I'm close to Vyšehrad.' He went on like this for a few more sentences, then suddenly said: 'Hang on, she's coming out. She bought another pot of chrysanthemums. And now… yes, it's just as I thought: she's going up the street. I'll call you again when I get a chance. I don't want to lose her…'

II

ONE MONTH before this, the ringing of the telephone interrupted the eight o'clock silence in the home of Ludvík Slaný, who began each morning by finishing the chapter that he'd started reading the day before. The journalist couldn't stand it when the world intruded on him during this reading time, even if it was only the miaowing of his cat. He usually treated these attempts at intrusion with contempt, knowing that if he gave into them his day would be ruined, like a sleepwalker rudely awakened during his nocturnal perambulations. Slaný's early-morning reading time was sacred. It was the antidote that allowed him to come back to life. After that, the world's slings and arrows could rain down on him, but they never truly hurt him.

That morning, the telephone rang for so long that, after a few ineffective curses, he rushed across the room, knocking a photo frame from a shelf in his haste. The frame fell to the floor and he heard the glass smash. He picked up the phone in time and answered nervously: 'Hello? … Oh sorry, it's you. Excuse me, I thought… No, you're not dis— Actually, I was just getting ready to leave… Lunch, today? Um, yes, I'm free… Of course, it would be my pleasure… It's not bad news, is it?… Okay, Filip, see you inside at quarter past twelve. And you'll book a table? Okay, bye.'

Ludvík picked up the pieces of glass and the frame and, in a flash of pain, he remembered the day he took that photograph of Zdeňka – a close-up of her beautiful Tatar face, or pre-Asiatic as he'd called it back then, at the beginning of their affair. It had been during that Sunday outing to Kutná Hora that he'd told her how much she resembled the Russian actress Tatiana Samoilova. And that wasn't just a line – he really meant it. With her high cheekbones, almond eyes, flowing curls and dark eyebrows… Ironic that it should have been a call from Novák that caused the clip-frame to fall from the shelf. Perhaps, after all, it was time to find a drawer for that picture of his girlfriend… or ex-girlfriend? He no longer knew what to call her, since nothing remained of that love affair but the broken pieces.

What did his editor want, calling him at home so early in the morning instead of waiting for him to arrive at ČT1? True, Filip Novák did not like mixing with lowly reporters, but he could easily have called Ludvík's desk phone later that morning and summoned him… He hadn't said much on the phone – a habit from the old regime. And although Ludvík Slaný told himself that nobody invited you to lunch if they wanted to reprimand you, he knew that it would be a long morning, waiting to find out what his editor wanted. Everyone who worked in the editorial department feared the summons to Novák's office on the third floor. Whenever someone was told to 'go upstairs', they would turn pale and ask if the boss had, by chance, said anything else?

Nope, nothing else. Maybe he has a surprise for you, the others would say, sniggering. Or maybe he just wants to let you stew…

Later, on the tram, as he reluctantly surrendered his seat to an old lady, Ludvík thought that perhaps it was a good thing he was so wary of his editor. It's never a nice feeling when you learn that a superior wishes to speak with you, but when that superior is Filip Novák the sense of unease takes on proportions difficult to imagine for anyone who doesn't work for him. Particularly when you have reason to believe that you are his *enemy*.

*

Novák liked to give the impression that he had been a regular at Na Rybárně for several months now. He had *his* table, in the best room. The boss wants to join the new era, to mingle his thoughts with the nicotine of ex-dissidents, his colleagues joked.

It was the first time Ludvík had ever been inside this restaurant. He was early. He walked down the half-dozen steps and – surprise! – saw Novák already there, standing up from behind the table and reaching out to shake his hand, an uncustomary smile on his face.

Behind him, along the painted wall, raged a sea at dusk. A whaleboat rode the waves, listing dangerously for the fifteen fishermen who sat inside it. Over time, those waves had taken on the yellowish stain of tobacco. One man stood in the boat, paddle in hand, on the lookout, but during the rest of the meal Ludvík didn't have a second to observe him, to see if he could spot the cetacean they were hunting, because Novák, being a busy man, gave him just enough time to order his food before getting down to business.

'I'm looking for someone with a logical mind… you know, someone with a good head on his shoulders. Someone who can think clearly and won't be distracted by a good story or some surprising revelations. And I think you are the rational man that I need.'

'For what?'

'A documentary of a particular kind, something close to my heart. It will require an unusual amount of time, thought and probably cunning too. It's a delicate subject and it'll need just the right approach. You'll see why.'

'If this is about politics or corruption… how can I put this?… I would rather not get…'

'Don't worry, it's nothing like that. But it's potentially even more explosive. Before I gave you the job, I wanted to talk with you and make sure you were up for it. You know what it's like in our line of work: people can be jealous, ambitious, and it's my job to manage those emotions. Did you hear the one about the journalist who committed suicide?'

Ludvík raised his eyebrows.

'He threw himself from the top of his ego… No, seriously, I want to be certain that you're committed to the project before I announce that you're in charge of this investigation, because the slightest hesitation could be exploited. I could write a book, you know, about conflicts between rival reporters.'

'And are you absolutely sure that—'

'It's your kind of thing, believe me. A story about a musical medium. None of the journalists who've investigated it up to now have been able to disentangle truth from fiction. You're probably familiar with the name of the woman at the centre of this story: Věra Foltýnova.'

Ludvík Slaný had never heard of her before, and yet he shuddered, as if certain names, when uttered aloud, release a sort of electric tension and what one might call a *memory of the future*, a vague intuition of what is going to happen. The shudder lasted only a heartbeat, though, and by the following heartbeat he'd forgotten about it and his attention was riveted on Novák, who was telling him about musical mediums. 'You know,' he said, 'since spiritism became fashionable in the second half of the nineteenth century, there have been those who claim to be visited by famous dead people, who continue their work and attempt to get recognition down here for their posthumous compositions. There was a spiritualist called Georges Aubert, in France, who said he was in communication with certain composers; there was Victor Hugo, who killed time during exile by communicating with the great men of history… And now, here, we have the case of this Foltýnova, who is fast becoming a media darling… Since we got freedom of speech, she's been telling anyone who'll listen that Chopin has dictated about a hundred pieces to her. She's not talking about a handful of compositions, which it would be relatively easy to fake. No, she's talking about a hundred. Mazurkas, ballads, études. We haven't been spared anything.'

'It all depends when she started composing, doesn't it? How old did you say she was?'

'Fifty-seven. Her father was Polish, so although she doesn't speak French, she is fluent in Chopin's native language. Supraphon sniffed an opportunity and they're making a *Best Of* CD of his supposedly posthumous output, some of which will be played by our Věra. The other pieces will be played by a famous pianist, as a way of drawing attention to the music. The foreign press is getting carried away and journalists from all over Europe have started turning up at her apartment. Only this month she's given interviews to the *Guardian* and *La Stampa*… Here, I brought you copies of them… So, yeah, this is already making waves in classical music circles. It hasn't yet reached the wider public, but those in the know are fighting over the truth. Camps are forming. The biggest camp is the sceptics, who are merrily pointing out the weak spots in what they claim are simple pastiches. Then there are the true believers, who are deaf to any arguments against this miracle: some of them are just people who need a fairy tale in their lives; others genuinely think that these "dictated" pieces are by Chopin himself… Between these two camps there's a grey zone of indeterminate geometry filled with fence-sitters of all stripes, the kind of people willing to follow the most cunning charlatans. Let's call this the swamp of the bewildered. But anyway, back to Věra Foltýnova. I'm not going to ask you what you think of her…'

'I don't think there's any point.'

'Do you know what she claims?'

'I feel like I'm about to.'

'That she's never had any musical training at all! An intriguing idea, obviously, and a lot of people have already fallen for it: fakers, cranks, mystics, gullible fools… but also some serious musicologists and musicians.'

'No musical training… Like, none at all? Not even a few piano lessons in childhood? That seems unbelievable…'

'I'm just telling you what's being said. And given the number of articles and interviews being published at the moment, I'd say the press, too, is being swept up in this craze. And you know the press as well as I do: it never does anything by half. All those journalists who – whether from a lack of means or a lack of professionalism – never have time to dig deeper to find out the truth of a story, who just swallow whatever bullshit they're told… Is that our job? No, for God's sake! We're not there to just regurgitate the lies we're fed! Some days, it's like we're back in the Middle Ages, with cabalists, witches and alchemists. If this woman really is Chopin's secretary, we need to demand proof. So, what I want from you is… a long documentary that will take the time to dismantle and dissect everything, and to expose the deception. Tear away the disguise. Prove that these pastiches really are fakes… You're a respected journalist in your scientific niche, but maybe you need to broaden your horizons, don't you think? To get out of your comfort zone for a while. You'll have the time you need, but the investigation has to be finished and the documentary ready to be shown before that Supraphon CD comes out. That gives us three months. There have been plenty of excellent documentaries made in less time than that… So what do you say? We can't just stand here and watch this happen. We have a duty to the public to set things straight. Let me be clear: we are not the prosecution here! Our role is to help people think, to question what seems set in stone. A serious documentary, one that will go down in history. I don't want to make a fool of a good woman, of course… Just to provide the public with the facts.'

'Okay, but I'm not sure how we can make people think, as you put it, and at the same time leave no room for doubt?'

Ludvík Slaný had been feeling nervous and uneasy for some time now. Sometimes he frowned, sometimes he scratched his chin or lifted up his glasses to rub his itchy eyelid. Something had awakened his suspicions. He felt nauseous, as if he were out there in that storm-tossed whaleboat with the men in the painting, as if this conversation were leading him on a long journey to an unknown destination.

'I would like us to get to the truth, to tear back the curtain and show the world the real Věra Foltýnova. To reveal the hidden side of the human heart, where shameful secrets are conceived. Believe me, this case seems to me symptomatic of a world without rules, of a ballooning egotism, a thirst for sensationalism… And perhaps, by extension, it also reveals the changes that have overcome our society in the last six years… The more I think about it, the more certain I feel that that is why this story is so captivating. As if the valve of a pressure cooker had suddenly exploded… Obviously, all this would have been impossible seven or eight years ago; this woman would have gone to prison before the press knew anything about it… You want another one?'

'Sorry?'

'Another drink?'

And while, without waiting for an answer, Filip Novák hailed a waiter to order more beers, Ludvík, waving away the plumes of smoke drifting from table to table, felt his suspicions aroused by his superior's flattering words at the same time as a faint drowsiness started to overcome him, as if the nicotine floating in the air were mixed with opium.

III

THEY ORDERED COFFEE. The restaurant slowly emptied. Outside, further up the street, the sun was making its first appearance of the day, but a shadow passed over Ludvík Slaný's face. He clumsily raised objections, citing all the work he was saddled with, the weeks it would take to be free of it. Besides, looking at this logically, wasn't the job he was being asked to do intrinsically biased, far from the objectivity he was being asked to display? Novák remained stubbornly determined, which started to make Slaný suspicious. He listened calmly as his employee became entangled in the convoluted threads of his own arguments and patiently waited for him to surrender. Novák was in no rush. He knew that he would eventually wear his opponent down.

The dregs slowly settled to the bottom of the men's cups; they had forgotten all about their coffee. Novák never directly addressed Slaný's objections. When at last he took a sip, he immediately frowned, a sign that the coffee wasn't very good, or perhaps that he was preparing his final attack, something along the lines of 'you know, I've given this a great deal of thought…' And that, indeed, was almost exactly what he said. 'I've thought about this, Ludvík, and I'm convinced that you're the right man – the only man – for this job…'

'But…'

'Let me finish. It's fine for you to start in two or three weeks, to give you time to finish what you're working on now. We'll find a way to arrange things. Or you can finish that other stuff later…'

Why was Novák being so stubborn about this?

'Because I know you, and because – as I already said – you're the one I need. Not because you're a detective but because I know you won't be fooled by the smokescreens that other people accept as reality. You'll lift up the veils one by one, until you reach the last one.'

'Assuming that some veils can be lifted,' sighed Ludvík, who was now regretting having answered the telephone that morning and starting to sense that he was being lured into some dishonourable scheme.

'You've probably thought, at times, that I didn't fully appreciate you, Ludvík. At least that's what I've gathered, because the walls of the editorial room have very sensitive ears. But I want you to know that it's not true. Contrary to what you might imagine, I feel no animosity towards you… You've already proven yourself an excellent muckraking journalist… Please don't make me flatter you too much; I've earned a reputation as a man who never compliments anyone and I don't want to lose that. But sometimes compliments are necessary, in situations like this one. I'm going to have another coffee. Will you have one too? Two espressos,' he said to the waitress, who was bringing them beers, confused by the drinking habits of these gloomy-looking customers absorbed in their verbal game of chess. 'Yes, you're a materialist. In this case, you see, the fact that you come from a family of communists is in your favour... Your mind is immune to the religious nonsense that is spreading everywhere and you're able to reason intelligently without slipping into the bargain-basement parapsychology that everyone's into at the moment. You were in the Young Communists, right? And... I know this probably isn't a very pleasant memory for you, Ludvík, but I remember the troubles you got into with Sholokhov thanks to your fascination with falsity and fraudulence. Am I wrong? You're attracted by duplicity and deceit, aren't you?'

When was the last time Novák had been wrong about anything? This was what Ludvík hated most of all in his boss: his sniper-like aim. His unerring ability to hit his adversary's Achilles heel to bring him down. The Sholokhov affair wasn't ancient history – six or seven years ago, perhaps – but how had Novák brought it up at such an opportune moment? That bastard, thought Ludvík, he's going to corner me... They fell silent then, as the waitress brought them their coffees, and Ludvík's mind was suddenly filled with bad memories. Why was it still so painful to him? Because, ultimately, he owed a deep debt to that affair... At the time, as a budding journalist at *Mladá Fronta*, he'd thought that the investigation was going to be his downfall, but a year later history transformed it into his saving grace. When Martynov, his section editor, had suggested he write an article on fraud in the arts, to fill the empty pages of summer 1989, he'd jumped at the chance. The piece had been accepted without difficulty but, on the day it was published, he was summoned to the managing editor's office. What could they want with him, the paper's rising star? He liked pastiches and frauds because he saw in them an artistic, contemporary reflection of the animal kingdom's most cunning survival strategy: deception and ruse. The chameleon's ability to conceal itself. The sole hiding in the sand at the bottom of the ocean... Ludvík probably saw in these methods a way to survive the regime of the time, but he kept that to himself.

The problem with his article related to the lines about Sholokhov, the author of *And Quiet Flows the Don*. According to some people, the Soviet writer hadn't written this book generally considered to be his masterpiece: he'd found the manuscript and claimed the credit for it himself, relegating its true author – a Cossack and White Russian by the name of Fyodor Kryukov – to oblivion. Where did the truth lie? Perhaps seduced by his admiration for successful deceptions, Ludvík seemed to give credence to the plagiarism theory. All he'd done was repeat some very old claims: namely, how could Sholokhov, at only twenty-two years old, have written the first volume of a work of such sweep and such erudition, knowing that he would deliver the following two volumes within the next four years? How could this womanizer who had never finished school have given life to a thousand characters, four hundred of whom actually existed?

The managing editor had hissed angrily: 'How dare you mention Solzhenitsyn's arguments? A traitor who was jealous that a real communist should receive the Nobel Prize before him! Don't you realize that Solzhenitsyn was trying to bring Sholokhov into disgrace?'

'But... I was careful not to mention his name...'

'Instead you quoted that idiot Medvedev and his book, which has been discredited by computer analysis of the work... I already have the Foreign Ministry on my back, thanks to you! And saying that everything Sholokhov wrote during the rest of his career was mediocre... well, that's just insulting.'

'I wasn't trying to... But, I mean, it's obvious, isn't?'

'What's obvious is that you are no longer employed by this newspaper. Finish your day and then leave... And think yourself lucky that I'm not disciplining you in any other way, out of consideration for your father's career.'

After he had spent a few months in the wilderness, events towards the end of 1989 overturned the order of things. That cursed article had given him quasi-heroic status and allowed him to find a job in public television; his stigmata had been transformed into a martyr's halo. How many others wished they had such a stain on their communist-era CV to give them a leg-up in this new world?

'... and so,' Filip Novák went on, 'I think your involvement in the world of fakes is not yet over. But don't worry, you have nothing to fear from that world now. Times have changed...'

Yes, that was true. What did he have to fear, now that everyone could express themselves with impunity? Why, then, did he have this feeling of doom? He should have been happy, because Novák was right: this story was temptingly to his taste.

We dream of projecting our ideal double into the world, whether to surprise ourselves or to amaze our dreamt-of soulmate. If Mikhail Sholokhov really had plagiarized a Cossack named Fyodor Kryukov, thought Ludvík, it was to show the world an idealized version of himself: the man he might have become if he'd finished school, if he'd only been blessed with talent. Or did he just want to achieve fame without having to work for it? Projection… Isn't he our worst enemy, the man we wish to be? He's a hitman who pursues us all our life, who kills us slowly, without ever opening fire. Our assassination lasts a whole lifetime.

What lack, what obsession, what inner catastrophe had driven Věra Foltýnova to make people believe that she welcomed Chopin into her living room and acted as a go-between for the worlds of the living and the dead? This investigation, thought Ludvík, would be a walk in the park if it weren't for a dark cloud on the horizon: in the opinion of several renowned musicologists and pianists, Mrs Foltýnova's pastiches were astonishingly clever, even confounding. If only they'd been able to find some small fault in those scores, some exogenous element never found in Chopin's work… Novák was quite frank about this (or at least he wanted to appear that way): the investigation was not going to be easy. That dark cloud threatened to unleash a rain of curses on him; Ludvík felt a strange certainty about this… And he was the one stuck with this unpleasant task.

'It's the perfect subject for you,' Novák insisted. 'You'll find the right arguments to counter our Chopinova's apostles. I have absolute faith in you.'

Faith? But what if Foltýnova had devised her plan to such perfection that even the most meticulous investigation wouldn't be able to dismantle it? What if she had accomplices? What if she was, in fact, merely a feminine screen concealing some wealthy plagiarist with the talent to compose *à la manière de* Chopin? The image of a poisoned chalice flashed through Ludvík's mind. The idea that this documentary would be impossible to make… He'd often chided himself for his anxious nature and had done everything he could to circumvent it, but now he felt it overpowering him, a sort of dark, tenacious trepidation. Was he walking into a trap? For months, he'd been fearful that Novák had found out the truth about Zdeňka and him, and had been seeking a way to get back at him. What if this documentary was the instrument of his vengeance? The banana skin? Novák was known for that kind of thing. He'd done it before to other journalists, giving them impossible assignments… For several weeks now, Ludvík had suspected the man sitting across from him of plotting his downfall. Had he found the ideal means to do exactly that?

What had put such an idea into his head now, rather than four, five or six months earlier? Ludvík had no answer to that. But how could Novák forgive him? He had become the lover of the woman who had dumped his boss! And the affair between Zdeňka and Novák had not been some mere fling. Zdeňka had admitted the fact to him once: 'I think about him sometimes, Ludvík. You have to understand: we lived together for three years. That's not something you can just forget.'

Zdeňka had sworn that nobody at the newspaper had a clue about her and Ludvík. Knowing her, however, he had reasons to doubt this; he sensed that she'd talked about it, swearing her listener to secrecy, of course, and that her words had been twisted or amplified on the grapevine before finding their way to the editor's office. It was true that Zdeňka no longer worked at ČT1. In order not to have to sit in editorial meetings and face her ex-lover and boss, as well as her new lover, she'd resigned after a few months; since then, Novák's heart had had time to stop aching, perhaps even to forget its pain... But could he be sure of that? Revenge is a dish best served cold, so perhaps Novák had waited, deliberately, before setting an ambush for Ludvík just when he had stopped fearing such a possibility? Was he about to pay a heavy price for the crime of being his boss's successor? Novák's insistence that he should take on such a delicate subject set him thinking. Ludvík wanted to pre-empt his boss by telling him that Zdeňka was leaving him too, so they were now partners in misfortune, abandoned by the same cold-hearted woman, and they should be on the same side... He wanted to tell him that she was like a nomad in the desert of love, never satisfied by the water she drank and, from the first taste, already thinking about her next oasis.

When the waitress came over to ask them if they needed anything else, her smile reminded him of what he considered Zdeňka's master smile – and the days when she still smiled at him – and this plunged him into sadness. What would he have left of her once their separation was complete? He wished he could steal that smile from her, keep nothing from their relationship but that image. He would have given anything to know whether she'd perfected it just for him or whether she'd used it with other lovers in her past. He still wanted to believe that it had been retired now and would never be used again. Had Novák, too, been the recipient of that sovereign smile, back when he and she shared everything, from a bed to their dreams?

Since their separation had started to seem inevitable, Zdeňka's face had transformed into one of those Noh masks: Ko-omote, the young woman with the impassive features.

Yes, the temptation to tell Novák point-blank that she was leaving him surged through Ludvík like a flash of lightning, and yet something held him back. What if Novák hadn't heard about their affair? In that case, telling him would be a ridiculous blunder. It would give his boss a reason to hate him, would rekindle the memory of a woman who was, for him, perhaps nothing more than a cold idol.

In that instant, Ludvík felt something fundamental change inside him. It was like nothing he had ever felt before. A decision formed. He was going to surrender to Zdeňka's master smile, which hovered in his mind, and make this documentary, even though he had no real reason to, even though his intuition was warning him not to. If it was his fate to live for a long time – a long time after his separation from Zdeňka Ustinova, a long time after Novák, a long time after 1995 – he would think back to this lunch with the man sitting across from him, motionless as a predator lying in wait, sipping his second coffee of the morning and hearing, without blinking, those few short words with potentially far-reaching consequences: 'Okay, Filip, I'll do it. Give me a few days off and I'll get to work. Any chance Roman Staněk would be free to work with me? I don't want it to sound like I'm setting conditions, but I'd really like him to be my cameraman.'

IV

Ludvík Slaný remembers every little detail of his first meeting with Věra Foltýnova. The morning he went to her apartment, he was accompanied by his cameraman and assistant, Roman Staněk, with whom – until then – he'd never had any problems. They had worked together harmoniously on other films and were bound by a feeling of mutual respect. He also knew that his cameraman was a fan of romantic music, an area in which his own knowledge was severely limited. And Roman Staněk had another gift that could prove important: he was a straightforward man, someone who simplified every situation. His colleague's life appeared absolutely crystal clear, without any complications at all. How did he manage it?

The 22 tram dropped them off in Jugoslávská, close to Londýnská, the street where Věra Foltýnova lived at number 57. Running perpendicular to Jugoslávská, it was largely residential, with few pedestrians. A hotel – the Luník – rubbed shoulders with various apartment and office buildings, some of them quite old, others less so. At the foot of number 57, Ludvík looked up at the third floor, dappled with the morning sunlight. So it was there, behind the windows of this stark building… He would have liked to spot a female figure, standing on the balcony and watching out for their arrival.

After glancing at his watch, he signalled to Roman: they weren't too early, so they could go through the entrance hall on the left. As they walked past the letterboxes, Ludvík scanned them until he came to FOLTÝNOVA. Only then did he truly believe it: thirty feet above his head lived a woman who claimed to be visited by a man who'd been dead for a century and a half. 'Well, she is a widow after all,' he joked as they climbed the stairs. 'She can make a new life with anyone she likes.'

They reached the third-floor landing. They rang the doorbell and heard the floorboards creak. Footsteps. 'Chopin's hiding under the bed,' muttered the cameraman, but then a key turned in the lock and the door opened to reveal a woman who looked even older than her fifty-seven years. 'Pani Foltýnova?' Ludvík asked, as if he didn't already know the answer.

'I was expecting you. Please, come in…'

Was it at that moment that Ludvík really understood what he had got himself into? Or was it a little later that strange morning?

'I was expecting you. Please, come in…'

She spoke those words of greeting with a humble smile, as if she had no idea that she was now a star of sorts. With her slightly eccentric flowery dress she looks like an Englishwoman, thought Ludvík as he sank into an armchair, eyes dazzled by the sunlight that blazed over the Luník Hotel, its backlit windows like obsidian pupils watching him. Yes, a working-class Englishwoman, modest and dignified, with a high-pitched voice, an irreproachable expression, and an attitude of distant respect. There was something distinguished about her, a lack of affectation. The apartment, as far as they could see, was in harmony with its occupant, with flowered wallpaper and, on top of the television set, a row of black-and-white family photographs arranged on doilies that she must have embroidered herself at some point. Above the door hung a small crucifix and a palm branch, while the shelf of the dresser was covered with religious knick-knacks. Ludvík smiled when he saw them, then his eye was caught by a photograph of a Black Madonna.

'My father took me to Częstochowa on several occasions. He's the one who gave me that picture… I was born Kowalski, Polish on my father's side… My mother was Czech. We moved into this apartment in '45… Before that, we lived in Ostrava, close to the Polish border and my father's hometown, Gliwice. My parents died a few months apart in the mid-Sixties, my father of a heart attack and my mother of grief. I decided to stay here. My children grew up within these walls. It's a very big apartment for one person, but I've never felt able to leave.'

(Ludvík smiled at this. Did she summon the dead to fill her empty apartment?)

It was perhaps while she was speaking these phrases in a monotonous voice, like someone reciting a passage learnt by heart, that – his eyes gazing at the flowers on the wallpaper and then at those on Věra Foltýnova's dress – he sensed that there was some disconnect between this woman and the idea he had formed when listening to Novák talk about her; as if this meeting in the habitat where she'd spent a large part of her life had somehow transformed her. Could this woman really be a con artist? A Machiavellian forger, driven by a lust for fame, who had fooled the world without ever giving herself away? The woman he was staring at was plain, unassuming, ordinary-looking. Something here didn't add up… The most surprising thing was how insignificant she seemed as she spoke to them, standing next to a pedestal table where two magazines of romantic stories lay, their pages splayed open. She didn't look like a swindler. Then again, she didn't look like anything in particular, not even the housewife she claimed to have been. A little too distinguished? Baffled, the journalist glanced at his cameraman, seeking confirmation, but Roman seemed miles away, on another frequency.

The living room was filled with a lingering scent of flowers, even though its only vase was empty. Presumably she had thrown away a withered bouquet not long before (just before their arrival, perhaps?) and its odour remained in the air. Lilac, thought Ludvík, before noting a little later, intrigued: but it's not the right time of year for lilac blossom.

It would have been an exaggeration to say that the flowery wallpaper covered every inch of the apartment's walls. Here and there, little frames broke up the uniform vegetation, some of them rectangular, others oblong, like portholes, through which little pencil-drawn faces peered out. Who were they? It hardly mattered. It was the style that held Ludvík's attention. Sketches in charcoal or Indian ink, created by a gifted hand, occasionally reminiscent of the illustrations of Alfred Kubin. These faces, strangely, had a frozen or mineral quality to them, a timelessness, that intrigued Ludvík. As if, just after being drawn, these beings had been petrified in their final expression.

'Do you have an artist in the family?'

She looked embarrassed.

'An artist? No… I like to draw from time to time… It's my hobby. I've always enjoyed drawing, ever since I was a child. These are portraits of my poor husband, and my children, too, through the years. My husband took photographs and I liked to sketch faces, expressions… I also like doing landscapes, in Indian ink. It's my favourite way to relax. I feel like I've been transported to another place.'

It was true, he saw now: there were not only portraits on the walls. And while the faces had something petrified about them, the landscapes, by contrast, were full of movement and electricity, as if animated by some mysterious tragedy. They looked like the work of a sorcerer. Rops, Munch… The drawings were bathed in a fantastical, baleful light that he found oddly compelling. It was hard to believe that the landscapes and the portraits had both been created by the same hand.

'I used to draw a lot as a child. I still do it now, but less often. It's the only affordable form of art, don't you think? My parents were far from rich, and as an adult I've always lived modestly, out of necessity. My husband didn't earn much, and in certain periods we were living hand to mouth… For a long time, I cleaned offices. When my daughter Jana was born, in 1970, I stopped working. The following year, I had Jaromil. I raised them myself… After my husband's arrest, I had to find work again. You know how it was… He wasn't in prison for long, but I had to find a way to pay the bills. When he came out, Jan was no longer the same man. His health, which was already fragile, had deteriorated due to the poor conditions and the pleurisy that he caught while he was incarcerated. Of course, he didn't get his old position back. He had to look for other work and it took him months to find a part-time office job. For my part, I accepted employment in a school cafeteria…'

She smiled at them.

'Curious, isn't it, that Chopin should have chosen me?' She looked pensive. 'I told you that when my husband came out of his prison he was badly weakened… He wanted us to emigrate. His dream was to live in West Germany or England. During his final months, he wasn't able to work anymore; he was bedridden most of the time. Have you noticed the little vibrations here? There are trains, under the ground. When they leave the central station, they go through a long tunnel, perpendicular to our street. The trains that head west… Jan spent most of his days lying down, so he had all the time in the world to pick up those vibrations. One evening, during a period of remission, he told me: 'Listen – that's the Cheb train. The one going to Germany. If I ever get better, we should get everything organized and take that train, don't you think?' He begged me and I promised. I swore to him that we would apply to emigrate, that we would try to get out of here. What would we have done in the West? I really don't know. I really wish Jan had been with me to experience the events of '89. It was a sort of victory for him, but he wasn't there to enjoy it…'

Silence.

'After my husband's death, I worked overtime to make ends meet. That was a sad, difficult period, even if our children were old enough to look after themselves by then. They helped me, but I found it hard. I was exhausted all the time, anxious about the future, and at last what had to happen did happen:

a ridiculous accident. I was cleaning tables in the cafeteria when I slipped on some orange peel. I fell onto the corner of a table and fractured several ribs... That was how I came to be bedridden for a long time, at home. In the first few days, any movement I made was painful. After a while, I was able to get up and take care of the apartment.'

Another silence.

'I suppose you could say that it was thanks to that orange peel that it all started.'

She fell silent once again and stared into space, as if reliving the time of the accident, and Ludvík wondered if she used to be pretty when she was younger. Later, when they were shooting the documentary, he would suggest that she show him some old family photo albums... He would have liked to X-ray her, to examine those spectral masses, some of them bluish, others diaphanous, inside her skull, to study the map of her brain until he could track down the location where it had happened, the secret place where the idea for this enormous con had first germinated, the insane idea that Věra Foltýnova, a cleaning lady with no musical training, would compose Chopin here, on this cheap piano with its yellowed keys like a smoker's teeth.

Ever since Ludvík had started listening to her, one question had been burning on his lips. It concerned that black upright piano, backing onto the living room's north-facing wall. Finally, intrigued by the instrument, he took advantage of a moment of silence, a lull in the conversation, to say: 'I thought you weren't interested in music. That you didn't know much about it. That's what you said in your interviews, isn't it? So how long have you had that piano?'

Věra Foltýnova did not seem fazed by the question. 'About twenty years, I think. When my mother-in-law died in 1972 she left it to us… Jan wanted to keep it. He thought maybe the children would learn…'

'So your mother-in-law played?'

'Yes. Quite well, in fact.'

'And you?'

'I started again, at my own pace, but I didn't take up lessons again. Back then, the children were still very young and I didn't have much time to myself. I would have liked to pay for them to take lessons, but we couldn't afford it.'

'Wait, are you saying that you used to play the piano, when you were younger?'

'I had a few lessons when I was about nine or ten, yes. A little belatedly, my parents decided that it was part of my education, so they paid for me to take lessons and I developed a taste for it. Once a week, I went to see a retired old lady who gave private lessons for some extra income. A widow. After the events of '48, my parents decided I had to stop; the lady was a former aristocrat and it was better for me not to be seen with her. Anyway, financially, everything became more difficult then. So I only had about eighteen or twenty months of piano lessons…'

'But you said in several interviews that you knew nothing at all about music, that you'd had no musical training at all…'

He emphasized the words *nothing at all*, but it would have taken more than that to fluster her.

'Does it really matter?… A year and a half of piano lessons, once a week, fifty years ago… At best I acquired some basic knowledge, which I quickly lost afterwards... When that piano was delivered to our apartment, I tried to recall what I'd learnt as a child. If only you'd heard how clumsy I was, the day my fingers touched those keys again! The kids kept interrupting me all the time. They were shouting out their nursery rhymes. It wasn't a pretty sight, believe me! It was a struggle for me to read music, so to say that I used to play the piano and that I was able to return to a certain level of proficiency would be extremely presumptuous on my part...'

As she'd fired off this little salvo of words, her mischievous pupils had shrunk in such an odd way that Ludvík, looking up from the piano and seeing the crucifix with its dried palm branch amid the wallpaper's field of flowers, abruptly changed tack.

'Forgive me if this question is too personal, but are you a believer?'

Her eyes opened wide at this unexpected query.

'I received a religious education from the nuns in Ostrava... Afterwards, of course, that was cut short, but – like my parents – I remained attached to Catholicism. Am I a believer? Yes, and I see no need to hide it. Not anymore. When I was young, I had to walk a long way to the convent in the mornings. I often miss the Ostrava of my childhood, and those early-morning walks. I could always go back there to live. The idea tempts me sometimes. But would the city now be the same as the one I knew? My father liked it there, but he was in his element: coal and steel. He was a mining engineer. If we climbed to the top of the slag heaps, we could see Poland, which had its own slag heaps... Do you know Ostrava?'

Ludvík shrugged.

'It's a curious town. There's something hypnotic about its strangeness... I'm sure you've heard about the overhead cables that transport baskets of coal above the gardens and streets... or that used to transport them, rather. I don't know if they still do. Sometimes, coke dust would fall from the sky onto the snow-covered pavements, and through the winter the snow would gradually turn black... The town was built over several mines, and some of the buildings collapsed. When I walked to school, I used to pass a very small church that was sinking into the ground beside the street. And the castle, which had been built on a small hill, was also being swallowed up. But the funniest thing, for us children, was the school's stadium: it was probably the only stadium in the world with a football pitch that sloped. Only a little bit – it wasn't visible to the naked eye. But it certainly made a difference which side of the pitch you played on. We girls were allowed to watch the boys play after classes ended, at the start of summer. It always made us laugh, watching those red-faced young men straining to run uphill when they thought they were on level ground.'

Ludvík and Roman didn't film that first meeting, they just listened. They agreed with Věra Foltýnova the time frame for their future meetings, the subjects they would discuss, and then they talked about documents they might be able to use: family archives, for example. They sketched out a shooting schedule... They could have left it there, but Roman wanted to get an idea of the piano's sound. From the look on his face, he wasn't expecting much. Smiling a little tensely, he asked the widow: 'Would you mind playing something for us, now? Something dictated by Chopin, for instance. The most recent piece?' She hesitated, muttering something about not knowing it perfectly yet because it had only been composed a month ago. Then, consenting at last, she lifted the keyboard lid, sat down and turned to them to announce, in a shy, almost apologetic tone: 'A mazurka.' When she started to play, Ludvík couldn't help shivering. What a singular melody... Like a long-forgotten memory slowly returning, these bars of music, supposedly sent from beyond the grave, had crossed through silence to disturb the peace of the living. The journalist found it hard to free himself from the impression that these musical phrases had not been composed here, in this room, and he grew annoyed with himself. He felt split in two, each half finding the other ludicrous... 'It's not bad at all, it really sounds like Chopin,' whispered Roman. When the last note had faded to silence, nobody spoke. At last, the cameraman managed to utter a few simple words: 'Thank you. We'll leave you now. See you next week. And thank you for agreeing to take part in this documentary. You weren't obliged to do it and we feared that...'

'I did hesitate before answering your request. And, since I didn't know what to think, I waited for Chopin to present himself so I could ask his opinion.'

'Ah...'

'He thought it was just what we needed. He convinced me to accept. He really wants his new compositions to be heard by as many people as possible.'

When he left the apartment building, Roman Staněk walked backwards along Londýnská, his cameraman's eyes feeling the need to find angles, to check the light levels for future shots.

He was probably tracing the trajectory of the sun above this street. He and Ludvík stood with their backs to the Luník Hotel, silently, their eyes fixed on the third floor of the building facing them, as if they hoped to catch sight of Frédéric Chopin's angular profile. Instead, it was Věra Foltýnova they saw pass by the window and glance down into the street… What if this documentary was not the trap he'd imagined it to be? Ludvík felt quietly reassured by their first meeting. Perhaps Novák wasn't trying to harm him after all? He felt sure that this story would bring certain difficulties, but perhaps not from the direction he had imagined… From where, then? He wanted to ask the cameraman about this, but the words died on his lips for fear his colleague would reply: 'Stop worrying so much, Ludvík. It'll be fine.' Roman was roughly the same age that Ludvík's father had been when he died: about thirty. Ludvík observed his colleague, who was absorbed in some calculation of angles or filters, his brow furrowed. When Ludvík's eyes rose back up to the third floor, the woman's figure had vanished, but a question came suddenly to his mind, a question he had never thought to ask before: when a heart stops beating, does the person's conscience, his stream of thoughts, end that very second? Or is there a delay, measured in seconds or in minutes? And, if so, what happens during that time? Had his father – of whom Ludvík had no memory, since he'd died only a few months after his birth – thought about his baby son, for instance, while his family was preparing to bury him?

'Roman, we have to find a way to trap her,' he said in a low voice. 'We have to put an end to this nonsense, all this stuff about talking to dead people.'

'Trap her? How do you mean?'

'What did you think of her drawings?'

'I don't know much about art. I thought she was pretty talented. Those landscapes are strange…'

'And the portraits?'

'Well, they definitely looked like the photos of the kids and husband on the mantelpiece.'

'There's one thing I wonder…'

'What?'

'Nothing. Just something that occurred to me. I'm going to give it some more thought. There's no rush.'

V

THE FOLLOWING WEEK, they went back to the apartment to begin filming the first interview. Until the last moment, Ludvík Slaný expected to get a phone call announcing that his interviewee was unwell or that she'd had to depart urgently for a funeral in a distant town, so their meeting would have to be postponed. He feared that she would get cold feet. He felt certain that she'd been aware of the journalist's scepticism, his suspiciousness of her gifts, and he imagined that she would call the whole thing off. He worried that she had understood the true intention behind his documentary: not to help her promote her CD, but to unmask her deception.

Nothing of the kind happened. By the time he left his apartment, she still hadn't called, and he jumped onto a tram somewhat reassured. Roman was waiting for him on Londýnská at the agreed time.

There was a sinking feeling in Ludvík's chest as he entered the widow's old-fashioned apartment. The framed drawings, the flowery wallpaper, the eternal scent of lilac with no apparent source, the gloom created by the half-closed curtains: everything here seemed to subsist outside of time, as if in the secret chamber of a pyramid.

Before they began the interview, Ludvík announced that he had a personal question to ask her. He looked embarrassed. 'It's like this…' he said.

He wanted to know if she would be able to put him in communication with a lost loved one; he would like to know that they were happy, beyond the grave. He was trying to put her at ease, to persuade her that he was a believer.

'I'm not the one who enters into communication, as you put it. *They* come to me… With Chopin, you know, it's always like that. And with the others too… The only power I possess is to receive their voices, their appearances, but I have often remarked that the simple fact of wanting something – or showing yourself to be open to it, if you prefer – can facilitate communication. They usually present themselves to me, however, rather than me initiating contact.'

So that's how she plans to get herself off the hook. She can sense that she might get cornered, thought Ludvík as she went into the kitchen to make coffee while saying, as if to herself: 'If a stranger ever comes to me, I'll let you know.'

'Please do,' he responded from the living room. He could hear the coffee brewing in the kitchen, which gave onto a little courtyard. 'It's important to me.'

Suddenly, in the silence that followed, they heard a cup smash. Fearing that she'd fainted, they leapt up and ran into the kitchen.

'It's nothing. It happens sometimes… I'm fine.'

She picked up the broken shards and mopped up the spilled coffee. She was white as a sheet. She kept repeating that it was nothing, but her pallor told a different story.

'Everything's fine,' she reassured them, even though they hadn't asked. 'It usually happens in the living room, when I'm resting or playing the piano, but this one came as such a surprise. I wasn't expecting it at all.'

'You fainted?'

'No, no.'

'Then… what happened?'

'You asked me earlier if I could get in touch with a person from your family. At that moment, I saw a boy of nine or ten years old who told me his name was Klement. It was hard to understand him; he didn't stay long. It happens when I'm tired; I find it very difficult to grasp what they're saying, to make the meeting last. It was like that this time, but I gathered that this person belonged to your family. You knew a Klement, I believe?'

He hesitated for a moment before nodding and answering calmly: 'Yes, that's right.' She described the young boy who'd appeared: he looked like he'd been a boy a long time ago… 'His clothes, his haircut… he had brown hair combed forward, with a fringe that came halfway down his forehead… Pale eyes under thick eyelashes, a lively gaze, regular features, a thin nose… The beauty of his face was slightly marred by his ears, which stuck out… As I explained, I saw him only briefly; he just had time to tell me that his name was Klement and that he was part of your family. Is this the Klement you were thinking of?' Ludvík nodded again. 'His outfit… I would guess it was from the beginning of the century, perhaps the Twenties. A white shirt and a plain, dark, three-piece suit.'

'So you never usually see children? Among your "visitors", I mean.'

'Very rarely.'

In truth, he didn't know this Klement character from Adam, but obviously he wasn't going to tell Věra that. He thanked her for helping him contact his loved one (and, in doing so, walking straight into his trap and confirming that everything this madwoman did and said was pure fantasy. Then his common sense corrected him: this level-headed, methodical madwoman).

Afterwards, the two men asked her to sit in a chair that they'd moved close to the piano, and Roman aimed two redhead lights at her. Věra seemed uncomfortable in the intense heat and brightness, but she said: 'I'll be okay, don't worry about me. Just arrange things the way you want them.' Ludvík then asked her to concentrate on a specific memory and to describe it in as much detail as she could: the moment when, for the very first time, an unusual contact was made with Chopin. (He almost said 'when you had the impression that an unusual contact was made' but stopped himself just in time, so that she wouldn't sense his doubt.)

'Unusual? You know, for me, there's never been anything unusual about contact with the dead, ever since I was a child… The strange, the unusual: in my eyes, it was always that the others couldn't see what I… I just couldn't understand that their capacities should be so limited!'

She was nine years old. A Sunday morning. Some time before, her parents had stopped letting her go to Mass. As soon as she opened her eyes that day, in the paleness of early morning, she noticed that she wasn't alone. A man with a very serious face was standing at the foot of her bed. Who could this be? She felt no fear when she saw him. She had a good feeling about this anxious-looking man, although she couldn't have said why. Perhaps because he was polite enough to wait for her to emerge fully from sleep before he began speaking. His face sparked no recognition in her. To judge from his clothes, he must have lived in a different era, probably the previous century. She had never seen anybody wearing that kind of frock coat. But why was he here, so early, at the foot of her bed? She guessed that the man was about forty years old, although at her age it was difficult to estimate how old grown-ups were. He spoke to her in a gentle voice and, to her surprise, not in her maternal language but in her father's... A day would come, he said, when he would need her. When that time came, he would appear again. It would take time, he didn't know how long; many years, undoubtedly. For now, she couldn't do anything for him because she was still too young.

The man did not introduce himself, probably because an adult does not announce his name to a nine-year-old child. Yes, he said, I will show myself when all the conditions have been met. This formulation intrigued her: what did he mean by the conditions being met? She didn't dare ask him, not because he intimidated her but because, in truth, she felt something like pity for this man with the pained expression, who finally smiled and said reassuringly: 'Don't worry, I won't ask you for the moon!'

Věra was so young, so unaware of everything that was happening in the world, that she nodded off, comforted by these words of kindness. She was accustomed to this kind of intrusion in her bedroom and there was nothing particularly unusual or affecting about this one, so she fell asleep in the cocoon of her sheets and drifted into the world of dreams until the first tram creaked along Jugoslávská and woke her. She could hear her parents' voices in the kitchen, but the man with the anxious face had gone. Intrigued, she wondered what he'd meant about coming back to see her in the future.

What began then was a long childhood Sunday. This was two or three months after 'victorious February' and she noticed that certain words like church and Mass were mentioned less frequently in her parents' conversations, although she had no idea why. But there had been so many things that intrigued her since she'd reached the age of reason…

When she got up, Věra told her mother about the visit, as she always did after meeting someone who had appeared out of thin air. Normally her mother listened attentively and cheerfully asked for details, but that morning her face was oddly sombre, as though her internal temperature had suddenly fallen. What was wrong? Her mother remained silent, and all day long the child was left bewildered, too timid to ask why. Had she said something out of turn? The visit she'd received that morning was not fundamentally different from any of the others… Was it just because the man had promised to come back? Had the visitor from beyond the grave committed some sort of sin by implying that he could, many years later, take a living girl for a wife?

Her father had gone to visit a sick cousin in Mělník and did not return until late afternoon. Věra saw him go into the kitchen for a talk with her mother but she couldn't hear anything of what they said. A little later, he took his daughter aside. He wished to speak with her. She sat on her little bed while her father stood in front of the window, backlit by the setting sun. He was silent, pensive, his eyes fixed on the parquet floor as if searching the knots and veins of the waxed wood for the best words to make himself understood. Spooked by this long silence, Věra began to whimper and her father put a hand on her shoulder. 'Don't cry, Veve! You haven't done anything wrong. Nothing at all…'

'Shouldn't I have seen that gentleman? Is he a bad person? Could he have hurt me?'

'Not at all, Věra, not at all. He didn't tell you his name, I suppose? You didn't recognize him?'

'No, he left without saying who he was… Is he wanted by the police? Is he a thief?'

For the first time, the little girl saw her father smile openly. She stopped crying.

'No, don't worry about that. But listen carefully, because what Daddy's going to tell you is very important. When this happened before, I asked you not to tell your friends or the teacher at your school about the people you "see", remember? Those other people can't see them and I don't want them to make fun of you or be jealous of you. The last time you told us about a visit like this, it was just before Christmas, wasn't it? About four or five months ago?'

'Uh-huh…'

'You know, in February, there were some big changes. Some of the new leaders are bad people, Veve. You have to watch out for them, because they have ears everywhere. Above all, don't tell anyone what you hear at home. We've explained this before: everything we say, as a family, must remain secret. Even if your teacher questions you. Okay? And… one other thing: the people you see, the ones who aren't alive… you must never tell anyone about them, apart from us. You understand? Not a word about any of your visits. Never at school. Never when you're with your friends, even if you're bursting to tell them. Because, for the bad people who are the new leaders, only the living exist. Dead people do not reappear, according to them, and if they find out that you've seen them, they might take you away to a madhouse… They'll say that you're a witch or that you're spreading lies. And your mother and I could go to prison for a long time, so we'd never see you again. Do you understand what I'm saying, Veve? This is serious. I'm certain that the State wouldn't approve of your visitors, and do you know why? Because the bad leaders can't catch or control the people who come to see you, and that would make them very angry… Nowadays, the State wants to know everything.'

The man who visited Věra Foltýnova that morning did not come back during her childhood, she calmly told the journalist as the camera recorded her. She stopped thinking about him and buried that Sunday in the deepest recesses of her memory. She also did what her parents told her: she never spoke of the apparitions to anyone, although that didn't prevent her father spending time behind bars later in his life. But that was a different story.

Four years later, bedridden with flu, Věra was leafing through some books. Her fever had started to abate, but she still wasn't allowed to get up or receive visitors. Her parents didn't get back from work until late afternoon and she had several hours to kill, alone in the apartment. After reading and rereading her comics, she had no means of relieving her boredom but to pick through the pile of books that her mother had left on the bedside table.

She grabbed the thickest volume: an encyclopaedia published *before*, as her father put it. He always punctuated the course of time with these little notches – *before*s and *after*s – that nobody else seemed to notice. In this instance, however, even young Věra understood what he meant by that – before the changes of 1948. So, to her eyes, the 1935 edition of the encyclopaedia stood out from the rest of the books like a little Atlantis, often drawing her curious gaze to its yellowed pages full of engravings, synoptic tables and grainy black-and-white photographs. So there really had been a time when people could write anything they wanted! She skipped from article to article, losing herself with the same delicious dread that she felt in the hall of mirrors at the fairground, where her reflection was surrounded by a crowd of alter egos. She felt her temperature start to rise again and was about to close the volume when suddenly she frowned and moved her face closer to page 274.

When her mother returned, she found the girl out of bed and strangely agitated.

'Why are you up? I told you…'

'Mama!'

'What? I'm not going to tell you anything else until you're back in bed.'

'Do you remember a Sunday morning, a long time ago? I told you how a man came to visit me at dawn, how he stood next to my bed and spoke to me.'

'Yes, I remember…'

On the table, volume 1 of the encyclopaedia lay open, and in the centre of page 274 was an old, black-and-white photograph. Věra pointed at it.

'That's him.'

'Are you sure? It could have just been someone who looked like him.'

'I'm sure. Besides, he was wearing old-fashioned clothes, just like those…'

Later, when she did some research on Chopin, Věra discovered that there were only two photographs of the composer listed in the archives. He had belonged to the first generation of famous men to be painted and then, towards the end of their lives, photographed. Chopin had gone from colour to black and white, from the ideal to what we call the real, in the same way as his first love, the singer Konstancja Gładkowska.

The first daguerreotype in which the composer appeared, in the middle of the 1840s, astonished Věra when she discovered it. Chopin was supposed to hold his pose for several seconds, but the result was what we might call a snapshot: he looks surprised, caught off guard, even though he had to stay still for quite a while without moving.

Credited to Louis-Auguste Bisson, the second picture dates from 1849, the final year of the composer's life. This was the photograph that resembled the man who had come to Věra's bedroom. It was this photo that she pointed at, still in shock at the idea that a famous composer had patiently waited for her to wake up before telling her that he would need her, later in life. In the 1849 daguerreotype, Chopin was wearing a thick, raw-silk frock coat over a black waistcoat and white shirt, a scarf tied around his neck. He must have been cold in the room where he was posing, hands crossed in his lap… or was he suffering? For a long time, Chopin had felt ill. Look at his eyes, filled with anxiety. He is miles away from that room where he waits for the camera obscura to swallow his image! He probably has a bad feeling, even more ominous than on other days, and it is during that dark premonition that the photographer orders him not to move from his chair while the film is exposed. The expression on his face is a cry of panic as he feels time running out.

When will he need her? As soon as the teenager discovered her visitor's identity, she started wondering this impatiently. When, and above all, why? How could a simple girl like her help a giant from the previous century? After that, Věra explained to the journalist, her impatience faded. The months passed, she grew into a woman, and she barely gave Chopin a second thought except when she heard one of his tunes on the radio. In those moments, she would remember his words.

There was nothing exceptional about those visits that she received. The dead probably just saw her as the ideal postwoman to deliver their letters to the living. She was so used to these visions that she was surprised to discover that other children did not experience them. For her, they seemed like cripples of a sort, cut off from part of the world. But she didn't want anyone to think her crazy, so she stopped telling people about her visitors after her father warned her of the consequences. She became extremely cautious in the way she spoke and acted, fearful that she might unwittingly give away some clue. And yet she wasn't harming anyone! Growing up, however, she learnt that harm was irrelevant; under this regime, everything was suspect. So she watched herself like a hawk, filtering her own words before speaking them. This made her taciturn, and of course she grew more isolated. Věra Foltýnova considered herself a double agent, in the service of two worlds that pretended not to know about each other. Those worlds intermingled, they got caught in each other's nets, but hardly anybody knew about that. She was one of the few. In her solitude, this was her great consolation: she wasn't completely unique. Her mother, too, had the capacity to see *them*. She never said a word about it, but her daughter had figured it out from conversations between her parents that she'd overheard. One day, when she was eleven years old, for example, she heard her mother say: 'I saw Pavel today. He feels sorry for us. If he were still with us, he would help us out. My poor uncle… But anyway, this is what he advises. He has given it some thought and he wants me to tell you…' So, no, Věra was not some fairground freak who would end up in a travelling circus. She and her mother perhaps both belonged to a mutant branch of *Homo sapiens*, who had developed a sixth sense, just as certain fish had grown lungs, aeons before, and ventured out of the water.

Věra Foltýnova paused, clearly moved by the memory of her mother. Then she began to speak again.

My mother didn't see as many dead people as I did. When she agreed to tell me about it, I realized that my capacities were far beyond hers. In terms of the frequency and quality of the contacts, I mean. My mother tried her best to forget that she had this strange gift. That was why she never liked it much when I told her about my 'visitors' – because it reminded her of her own condition when all she wanted was be normal. Now I think about it, I suspect all that stuff worried her. She felt guilty at passing on to me something shameful, perhaps even harmful.

And there was something else too: she was never happy about me talking with dead people from our own family. 'How do you know that?' she would ask me sometimes, when I had unknowingly slipped into the realm of secrets. What I heard was: 'You should never have learnt that.'

In my defence, I became a master at keeping secrets. How the State would have loved to have an army of little Věras on its side! My poor mother… Over time, I learnt to keep most of my 'abnormal' encounters to myself, and in the end I must have seemed like a stranger to her. Absurd, isn't it, to become strangers to each other when we were cursed with the same ability? And yet that's exactly what happened, little by little.

'My mother died relatively young, at the age of sixty-three. She didn't live long enough to find out whether the composer whose photograph was in the encyclopaedia would return to seek my aid. She never came out and said this, but I think she would have loved to know what he wanted from me. Perhaps it would have given us poor 'abnormal' women some of our pride back.

When my husband died, in 1984, I had to look after the children on my own. Without his salary, it was hard for us to make ends meet. At the school cafeteria where I worked, my job was to clear and wipe the tables after meals. One day, I slipped on some orange peel and broke several ribs when I fell onto the corner of a table. Nothing too serious, but it was very painful and I had to stay at home for several weeks.

After two weeks they took off the plaster from around my torso and little by little I began to look after the apartment again. I wasn't stuck in bed anymore, so I could do more than just read and watch flies. When they came home from school, my children would help me to clean the house and make dinner.

During the day, though, when they were away, I had nothing to do. And so, one afternoon I lifted the lid of the piano and touched the keys. When I tried to play it, I realized that I'd forgotten everything. My poor hands couldn't do anything right anymore. I'd lost the little dexterity that I'd acquired during the short period that I played as a child. I would have liked to take lessons, since we'd inherited that piano, but with two young children I could never find the time. Besides, I couldn't afford to pay for lessons.

Was this unplayed piano a Trojan horse? I would often look at it, with the lid lowered and that vase that you can see on top of it – an old wedding gift – and the framed photos. The instrument reminded me of that Sunday morning visit in my childhood and the promise the visitor had made to find me again, later in my life, but it was so long ago! What did I expect? Although I had believed him when he gave his word, at times I was seized with doubt. What if I died before the visitor returned? How could I help him anyway? Most of his compositions were for the piano. Could his promise possibly have anything to do with this out-of-tune instrument? When I thought about my life, I had a low opinion of myself. My parents were dead, I was a widow, I had a boring job, and I couldn't even provide my children with the life they deserved. And now I had broken several ribs after a ridiculous accident, so I'd been stuck at home for weeks.

It was a strange thing, this forced inactivity. I was normally so hyperactive, so rooted in reality, but now I began to philosophize. I started to wish that I had the master key that would let me open every door to that world. Most of all, I wanted to understand it. And to have access to those millions of rooms where my peers lived, feasted, seethed with jealousy, loved and punished one another.

For some time now, fragments of melodies had been playing in my mind. Unfinished, imprecise, like reflections on the rippled surface of a lake. I put it down to my prolonged inactivity, all those days spent lying on my sofa: my body was idle, so my imagination had begun inventing tunes to pass the time. Those snatches of melody would fill my mind and then dissolve, like little white clouds in the vast blue sky. Some of them were melancholic, others quite cheerful. They were brief musical phrases, but some of them were genuinely beautiful, which amazed me. Then they left me. I forgot them. I thought perhaps I wanted to write music. But the oddest thing was that these melodies weren't… well, they weren't really my style. I certainly didn't suspect that these scraps of music hinted at anything more than a late-flowering desire to be a composer.

So, one afternoon, I lifted the black piano lid and tried to pick out a melody that had come to me. It must have been about two o'clock and I had quite a long time before the children came home. Tinkling the keys randomly, I was annoyed when I realized that my mind had either erased or buried those musical memories. I tried to remember the names and positions of the notes on the stave; to read the gobbledygook on my music stand. From time to time, something would glimmer and sparkle in my head, and I thought perhaps all was not lost.

And then it happened. I told you the other day that I perhaps owed everything in my life to that orange peel that I slipped on in the cafeteria. It happened when I sat at the piano. Suddenly, my hands started to travel along the keyboard. To play! I was shocked to see that my fingers had become so agile, that I couldn't control them anymore. The melody produced by my hands was completely unknown to me. Someone was playing through me, but who? There was nobody there. I was used to visits from beyond the grave, but even I was terrified by this, because I could feel no other presence in the room. I must have played for twenty or thirty seconds and then my hands stopped moving. I flexed my fingers, one after another, to make sure that they were obeying me again. They had become illiterate once more.

It was then that I saw him, as clearly as I see you now. Standing with his elbows on the piano. He hadn't changed since the morning of his visit thirty-seven years before, presumably because he was from a place where time does not exist. Had I sent him some sort of signal, a few minutes before, when I lifted the piano lid, a signal that had alerted him and brought him to me? When I think that I tried to sell the piano, just after my husband's death… Luckily, after seeing the instrument, the potential buyer asked for some time to think it over, and never came back. It had been a bitter blow at the time, because we needed the money to survive, but then the situation became a little easier and the piano stayed where it was.

Chopin looked just as anxious as he had on his previous visit, when I was only nine. Thirty-seven years had passed since then, for me: thirty-seven years of joys and disappointments. Thirteen thousand five hundred days of getting up and going to bed, of hoping and fearing, and all those layers of memories in between had not blocked out the image of that distant Sunday. He was wearing the same frock coat as he had the first time, probably the same one that you can see in the second photograph. He smiled wanly and spoke to me. 'I promised you once that I would come to see you again. You were a child. Do you remember?'

That was how it all began. As I told you, I've always been visited by dead people, for as long as I can remember. But I need to make it clear that, in my childhood, that type of contact was easier and more frequent. Family members, friends of my parents, people from the neighbourhood and quite a lot of strangers who didn't bother introducing themselves and didn't seem to want anything in particular. Most of the time they didn't say anything, and our meeting seemed pointless; they were just like passers-by that you might see on the street, people you wouldn't even think of talking to. When my visitors spoke, I heard them better than I do today; our worlds communicated without any interference back then. That is no longer the case. With the passing years, we slowly lose our hearing and our sight. There are periods of good weather, as I call it, when everything seems clear, and I can see and hear the other person quite easily, but most of the time our communication isn't good or it doesn't last long. It's a bit like receiving a telephone call: sometimes, there's static on the line or you lose the signal completely, for no apparent reason. It's the same thing with my visitors.

'Do you remember?' he said.

'I found out who you are, afterwards. You promised to come back when you needed me. That was thirty-seven years ago. Quite a long wait.'

'I'm sorry. Where I am, there is no time. But I do need you.'

'You need me? But I don't understand. What can I do? Who am I, other than the person who can see and hear you at this moment?'

'That's the important thing. Don't you realize? Very few people have the ability that you have.'

'All right. So now what?'

'I would like you to take dictation of certain pieces that I've composed since my death.'

'But I don't know anything about music! I can hardly even read the notes. A musical score is like Chinese to me! Do you really think I'm the right person to…?'

'Everything will be fine. We have time. We'll learn to work together. If you want to?'

'I'll probably make so many mistakes. You'd be much better off with a professional pianist.'

'No. We've thought about this.'

'*We?*'

'Myself and a few other composers like Liszt and Ullmann, who continue to compose. We think that a skilled pianist or a musicologist might want to *arrange* what we transmit to them. You won't. You are free of that kind of pretension. Besides, a composer or an interpreter would be too focused on themselves and their career. I prefer to deal with someone like you, whose ego is modest and who has plenty of time. Shall we try the first exercise?'

He must have known that I was at a loose end, particularly that afternoon. Strangely, I've always struggled with early afternoons; that time of day makes me feel slightly depressed, incapable of doing anything. On that particular day, I was downhearted, thinking about my husband and the life we could have had if he hadn't become ill and had all those problems with the StB. I was still in that melancholic state – a Chopin kind of feeling, if you will – when I agreed to be his secretary.

And so, without any preparation, I started taking dictation. He was very patient. He understood that the early stages of our collaboration would be laborious. If this was a horse race, then I was some old nag whose hooves kept getting stuck in the muddy ground of notes, tones, keys, staves. Despite all my misgivings, I was proud to have been chosen. He disappeared when my daughter came home from school, and I immediately felt empty. I told my daughter that I had indigestion and went to lie down in my room. I must have slept for two hours. When I awoke, it was time to make dinner. The children were worried. 'What's wrong, Mama? You're pale, you should go to see the doctor.'

Ah, if only they'd known! No doctor could have cured me of what had happened to me in their absence. Writing down music without really knowing what it all meant… It was only later, after having taken a few more lessons, that I was able to start playing.

After a pause, Ludvík said: 'What did he dictate to you that day?'

'A mazurka. That day, and in the days that followed. I would say it's the best of the twelve that he's sent me over the years.'

'We'd like to get some footage of you playing the piano,' said Roman Staněk. He looked questioningly at Ludvík as he said this, and the journalist nodded. 'It'd be good to hear you playing the first piece he dictated. When was that, exactly?'

'The twenty-seventh of March 1985. You know, even though I know the pieces by heart, I worry that I would make a mess of it. I don't think I have the necessary talent to…'

'I understand. Then perhaps you'd let us hear it for ourselves, off camera?'

Věra nodded and, as she sat down at the piano, Roman discreetly signalled to Ludvík that the camera was recording.

She hit a wrong note, then stopped after a few bars and started over. After that, she played seamlessly. The music moved like the tide, the pace varying in Chopin's famous *tempo rubato.* The piece lasted no more than three minutes, but it was long enough for Ludvík to feel overwhelmed. Thrilled by the two journalists' respectful silence, she then played an even shorter piece, but the spell was broken.

Ludvík wanted her to play the mazurka again, but he didn't dare ask. Despite Mrs Foltýnova's clearly limited technique, the music had plunged him into a singular state, reminiscent of light hypnosis. Certain phrases of Rachmaninov's Piano Concerto number 3, which he often listened to, tended to induce a similar state; about ten minutes after the beginning of the concerto, he would find himself floating alone on an ocean, then Zdeňka's face would appear and she would tell him that she was leaving him. That passage acted as a sort of balm, because he no longer felt any sadness, only a persistent melancholic intoxication. It was like dawn on the marshes, when birds flew up through the mist. Ludvík could detach himself from the things of this world and see his own existence as if from afar, like a cottage at the end of a valley. And this mazurka *à la manière de* Chopin had engendered a similar melancholy inside him.

'I have one more question... Did Chopin tell you, that day, why he was so determined to re-establish contact with the living?'

Hearing this question emerge from his mouth, Ludvík became annoyed at himself for playing by the rules of her game, for letting her believe that he was taking everything at face value.

'That day, no. We were too busy tuning our violins, so to speak. We were trying to find a way of communicating. In the end, he decided to dictate the notes to me rather than making me play them... But one day later, he did tell me that I should make the people around me hear his new works. He didn't want it all to be in vain. He didn't want to put me through all of that for nothing.'

'How long was it before you went back to work?'

'I stayed at home for more than a month.'

'And during that month, did he visit you again?'

'Of course. I think he came every day, apart from weekends, because the children were here then.'

'*Came?*'

'I was never the one who initiated a meeting. It was always him. You can't summon a dead person.'

'I'm sorry. So... once your convalescence was over and you were back at work, how did you manage to maintain contact with your new visitor?'

'The meetings became more spaced out. I didn't mention them to the children... But since I worked at a school cafeteria, I never got home very late. It was generally three o'clock, or three-fifteen at the latest, and that left me enough time at home, before their return. Also, at the start of the year, I'd been able to exercise my right to the State pension. Because I was widowed, and because I'd raised two children, I was eligible to receive it earlier than normal.'

There was something charming about this woman with her flowery dresses, thought Ludvík. An old-fashioned quality, noticeable in some of the expressions she used – 'exercise my right to the State pension', for example – that took you back, mentally, to the blessed days when you were told that everything was going to be all right.

VI

THIS MUCH WAS OBVIOUS: Věra was an Alice who had built her own wonderland, a place where she could live happily ever after. She had even told them that she would sometimes find herself in the presence of dead animals – cats, wolves, even (why not?) leopards – who stood before her, meek as lambs. So she was responsible for reintroducing wolves to this Bohemian town, and for releasing African predators into its streets… Such were Ludvík's thoughts as he exited the apartment building. Anyone questioning this woman in a superficial way could easily draw from her words a disturbing impression of coherence. Her system had its own logic, as if she'd spent a long time thinking about it, and it was surprisingly difficult to catch her out, never mind unsettle her. Intriguingly, Věra Foltýnova seemed to believe her own story; to her, it all seemed straightforward, inarguable. She clearly felt at home amid this nonsense and Ludvík kept wondering how she could manage to keep up the pretence to such an extent. She wasn't a charlatan or a composer, she was an actress. A peerlessly brilliant actress.

There was something disconcerting about her self-assurance. What would a police detective think, in his place? Did criminals always appear so convincingly sincere when producing their fake alibis?

'Of course,' the cameraman replied evasively. And then, a few seconds later: 'Why wouldn't she be sincere?'

Ludvík shot him an amazed look but said nothing. He'd been moved by that mazurka she'd played. And yet he'd been warned by everyone he talked to about Věra Foltýnova: 'There are at least a hundred of us – maybe two or three hundred – capable of writing this kind of thing... Don't let yourself get sucked in. Don't react like a child!' But the truth was he'd been impressed, not by the Chopinesque nature of what he'd heard – he really wasn't in a position to judge that – but by the intrinsic beauty of the piece, which had blown him away.

There was no doubt in his mind that this woman was incapable of having created those musical phrases. If she'd been motivated to compose, she would have done it in her youth. You didn't wait until you were nearly sixty before suddenly displaying signs of genius. But in that case, who *had* written that music? He slowly moved towards the idea that she was shielding someone else. A composer, an imitator who, for whatever reason, wanted people to hear his creations while remaining anonymous, at least to begin with... One of those two or three hundred people in the Czech Republic who were supposedly capable of producing Chopin facsimiles. These thoughts flooded his mind, midway between intuition and certainty. Yes... And what if Věra Foltýnova were only the figurehead of a much larger scheme? What if she were the candid, esoteric, romantic face of a completely rational and prosaic enterprise to make money out of people's gullibility? Wouldn't the release of an album and the media hype that accompanied it (in which Ludvík was participating, he thought bitterly) be sufficient motivation for such an elaborate con? It was human nature, wasn't it, this eternal ballad of truth and falsehood? Recruit a gifted musician, create a 'mystery' that transcends the frontier between life and death, and mix well: riches would rain down on you in return. But that would require the lead in this shadowplay to be a seasoned actress that nothing and nobody could faze, which seemed to be the case up to that point. What he needed to do was set some traps and wait for her to trip their jaws. And never let her go… Already, she'd confessed that she wasn't completely ignorant of music, in contrast to what she'd claimed in her first interviews, and that contradiction was far from insignificant. She had slipped out of that particular trap with the skill of a Houdini, but there were surely other lies that he could expose… He was going to check every declaration she had made – and he had a lot on his plate, because this woman liked to talk. All the same, he was surprised by how naturally she answered his questions. Either she believed absolutely in what she was saying, or she was an expert at dissimulation and manipulation. Did Alice truly believe she was in wonderland? Ludvík Slaný wished he could wash away the emotions that stirred inside him that day as easily as he might wash away a layer of dirt.

There were, he thought, two primary emotions at war in his heart. On one side, he wanted to expose and dismantle the deception; on the other, he felt himself drawn towards it by something that went beyond reason. He was a ship's captain spying an island that didn't appear on any map. It was something sacred and ancestral, something he would have struggled to define, so alien was it to the values that had guided him since he'd become an adult. Something that made him ache deep inside, as distant and imperious as a seasickness that leaves you utterly wrung out.

As soon as he got home, the telephone started to ring. His mother needed him to come and fix something; it was really nothing, she swore, as usual, and there was no rush, but whenever he had time… He decided to go there and attack the problem now, without waiting. At the end of this day that had left him depressed and disoriented, he would at least have the simple pleasure of helping someone. Less than an hour later, he parked his car near her house on a street in Smíchov.

His mother had not been lying: the repair was very simple, and he was finished in no time. She was the most helpless person he had ever met when it came to dealing with the small misfortunes of domestic life. She wouldn't let him leave without having some coffee and a few slices of strudel from the pâtissier Ovocný Světozor. 'I bought it this morning, after going to see my friend Klara. Do you remember Klara, from Kladno?'

He hadn't forgotten Klara – his mother had probably mentioned her to him about a thousand times – and, hearing the chime of her name and the name of the small town where she was from, both of them beginning with the letter K, his mind flashed back to the question he'd asked Věra Foltýnova and the boy called Klement she claimed to have seen. He'd put her to the test. And perhaps, after all, there had once been a Klement in the family? Now would be a good time to check.

'Someone called Klement? Not that I know of... Why?'

His mother's question wrongfooted him.

'Oh, no reason. I just read it in a list of names when I was doing some research at the television company... A man called Klement Slaný. So I just wondered if...'

'Slaný is a very common name, you know.'

'I know. But he came from the same region as Papa,' he invented.

'Olomouc? No, it's not ringing any bells. He never mentioned a Klement to me. So what was he doing, in your archives?'

'Nothing special. Forget it. I just wanted to check.'

Suddenly, he felt an immense relief, like a gust of wind blowing away the emotions that had oppressed him for the past few hours. Ludvík had methodically cross-checked the story and it was bogus. Foltýnova had been bluffing. She would probably claim that this Klement had lived in the seventeenth or eighteenth century and continue to string him along, but who cared? She had fallen into the first of his traps and he felt proud of himself. Comforted by the idea that she was the *enemy*. He couldn't let himself be fooled by this woman's apparent sincerity. He needed to keep in mind that he was dealing with a born actress, willing to do anything to protect her story. Well, he was going to show her that he was nobody's fool.

'So how are things with you and Zdeňka? Have you patched things up?'

His mother's question, fired off just as he was about to leave, caught him off balance. Oh, he knew exactly how things were with him and his girlfriend, soon to be ex-girlfriend; he knew there was no patching up their endlessly ending love affair; but it was such a delicate, painful matter and he couldn't talk about it to this old lady who had been hoping for so long, without truly believing, that one day she would be a grandmother.

'I think she's decided to live somewhere else instead of coming and going twice a week. I think she's gone for good now. That's life…'

'Shall I try to talk to her?'

'No, thank you. That's the last thing I need.'

'She's not in love anymore?'

'I'm sure she is. Just not with me.'

'And… do you know who with?'

'Yes. With herself. With her own navel. Her career. I haven't understood her for a while now. For the past year, that's all she's talked about – herself and her career. We're just not close anymore. She's obsessed with journalism and her life as a journalist.'

He didn't say anything else, and neither did she. Her 32-year-old son was single again, and her hopes for him were dying. What would his father say about it, if he were still alive? It was better to end the discussion before his mother started to weep.

The moment he opened the door to his apartment, Ludvík noticed her signature in the air. Zdeňka's perfume, Black Satin. She must have made a lightning visit while he was gone. He soon spotted a few objects that were no longer in the same place, a few drawers left half open. She had some sort of sixth sense that allowed her, almost every time, to slip inside his apartment when he wasn't there. As if she were monitoring his comings and goings somehow… She had probably come to pick up some bed linen, some winter clothes, a file that she'd left the last time she was here. Sometimes her interminable departure would set his nerves on edge, while at other times her hesitation gave him a vague and painful sense of hope. She didn't want to leave definitively. Every time, she left behind some excuse to come back, but in that case why didn't she wait for him to return? Why never drop by when she knew he would be here? He wasn't ready to break the enchantment she had cast upon him three years before. A sort of irresistible gravity kept him in her orbit. Even now, he found himself checking the tables and shelves to see if she'd left him a note. Then he became irritated with himself and gave up the search.

Nothing happened that evening, nor the next day. But the day after that, as he was preparing to go out, the telephone rang. He thought it was her. Or no, perhaps it was his mother. Oh well! What did she need this time? He really wasn't in the mood…

'I don't need anything, don't worry. I just wanted to check how you were.'

'Hmm…'

'Oh, and to tell you that I got a call from your Uncle František. I hadn't heard from him for a while. He's not doing too well.'

'Ah…'

'Do you remember when Papa used to talk about his brother Jan, who died very young?'

'Vaguely.'

'Well, František told me something I didn't know. As a little boy, Jan took a dislike to his name. He hated it so much that he forced his family to call him Jan. Legally, his name remained Klement, but everybody called him Jan and talked about him as Jan, to the point that his real name was more or less forgotten.

He thought it sounded good: Jan Slaný. Anyway… as you know, he died tragically when he was eleven years old.'

After hanging up, Ludvík stood like a statue for a long time, staring out the window at the slate scales of the bell towers in the golden shimmer of morning. He was shaking slightly. Everything would have been so simple if only he hadn't asked his mother that question…

'At that moment, I saw a boy of nine or ten years old who told me his name was Klement.' He thought back to what the supposed medium had told him. *At that moment…* Brown hair combed forward, a fringe that went halfway down his forehead; that was how Věra Foltýnova had described him. Pale eyes under thick eyelashes, a lively gaze, regular features, a thin nose and ears that stuck out from his head… Oh, if only his mother could show him a picture of a blond Klement, completely different from that description, how much better he would feel! Jan-Klement had gone out onto a frozen lake at the beginning of winter, but the cold had not had time to finish its work and the thin ice had cracked and collapsed under the boy's weight. From a distance, his two younger brothers saw him stagger then suddenly sink out of sight. Terrified of suffering the same fate, neither of them dared try to rescue him, and they would grow up with a feeling of guilt, the embers of which would occasionally flare red even years later. After the tragedy, everybody tried not to talk about Jan-Klement.

That was all his mother could tell him. For a photograph, he would have to wait until his uncle found time to dig through his chests full of memories. And, even then, it was possible that no portraits remained of the dead brother.

For a moment, Ludvík was reeling and ready to admit that Věra Foltýnova had scored a point, but then his rational mind rebelled. After all, it made no sense when you actually thought about it! Why would a dead boy introduce himself using a name that he'd hated when he was alive? Anyway, the whole thing was ludicrous. The dead rest in peace and they have nothing more to do with us. That woman must have randomly chosen a common name, calculating that a Klement was bound to turn up somewhere in the family, even if it meant having to dig deeper. Go back three or four generations, and you'll find a Klement or two in every family, she must have thought. As for the photograph, Ludvík hesitated, then finally called his mother back. Tell my uncle not to bother looking, he said, probably because he was afraid that one day he might have to face the black-and-white features of a boy with brown hair combed forward, a fringe that went halfway down his forehead, pale eyes under thick eyelashes, a lively gaze, regular features, a thin nose and ears that stuck out from his head.

PART TWO

VII

A GREAT DEAL could be written about the relationship between the press and the secret services in an authoritarian country, where journalists are considered auxiliary troops, useful for providing favours which can – in certain circumstances – be returned. A great deal could also be written about the transitional periods, the interregna, when an authoritarian regime gives way to an embryonic democracy, as is the case in our story. The new rules have not yet been clarified or are being applied only sparingly. In that tectonic shifting between civilizations, many things are permitted that ought not to be. Everything is in flux. Names are changing. Overnight, some men switch sides while others are sidelined. The new order wants nothing to do with them. What have they done to deserve such ostracism? That is not always clear. Some, presumably, served the previous regime with a selflessness that the new era condemns. Those men and women will now have to find another job, perhaps even move to a different country. They must start again from scratch.

At the age of forty-five, Pavel Černý, newly divorced, had responsibilities – child support to pay and a pronounced sense of his duties as a father – that made it impossible for him to leave his homeland. Besides, where could he go? He was a prisoner of his language and his past. Even the Russians wouldn't want him. He didn't even feel capable of changing his profession; in his own way, he felt an emotional attachment to it. Quite simply, he no longer served a State, an ideology; from that point on, he was a sort of secret service for individuals. He became a private detective.

Part of his skillset was innate, a natural gift: he never forgot anything. Not because he was a holder of grudges, but simply because his memory had a freakish capacity to store information, as if nothing – or hardly anything – was ever deleted once it entered his brain. A synaesthete of the first order, he could have been a great pianist, like Richter, or a brilliant mathematician, or a cutting-edge scientific researcher, venturing towards the horizon of the human mind, exploring new frontiers of knowledge... He could have enjoyed the satisfaction of being the first person to cut a path through the wilderness of the unknown and to describe what he saw there; he could have roughed out a whirl of explanations, hypotheses... But he didn't do that either. He preferred to serve the State, because – after he was orphaned at a tender age – the State had effectively been his mother and his father. Quite early in his life (was it at the orphanage or at school?), he had amazed the adults around him with his abilities. They'd made him an exemplar, distinguishing him from the others, the lumbering herd who had to sweat and concentrate to remember anything. His memory was photographic; it was a sponge. When asked, he could recite a poem *in extenso*, as if he were reading it from a page. In fact, that was essentially all he did. He was a one-man library. His classmates liked him and used him for his gift, but at the same time they feared him, did their best to avoid him. So much so that Pavel Černý quickly discovered the meaning of solitude – not the kind that people seek out and desire, but the kind that surrounds a leper when he enters a town, waving his rattle. Was it really a gift, what he had? Or was it actually a handicap? This aura of witchcraft had never left him, and perhaps it had benefited him, ultimately; at twenty, he'd been recruited to work for the State, and not in just any capacity: he became part of the war against the enemy within. His job was to foil, stymie and expose the opposition. To monitor the germination of plots so that they could be smashed as soon as they were put into operation. He did not want anyone to attack his new parents, the State, which he thought of as an old tree, its roots plunging ever deeper under villages, neighbourhoods and side streets. Deep into men's souls. Unlike most other sectors, the secret service never suffered budgetary cuts, and Černý always had everything he needed. Like his colleagues, he could count on a never-ending supply of informers. Ambitious youngsters who saw betrayal as a ladder; bitter, jealous misanthropes who denounced others out of *schadenfreude*; and – the smallest group but also the most formidable – the pure of heart, whose ears were never idle.

Among these various subspecies of informers was one young, budding journalist who aspired to join the national broadcasting service and was prepared to do anything to achieve his ambition. His name was Filip Novák. He never had to be recruited; he was a willing volunteer. Labelled an upstart and a braggart, he had a talent for inserting himself in all kinds of circles and gaining people's trust. Pavel Černý appreciated the zeal and particular gifts of this man codenamed 'Bilek', who would sometimes hand-deliver letters to him. Agent Černý had taken care to hide these letters, along with many other sensitive documents, just before the collapse and dissolution of the StB, so that he could use them when the time came. He must have had about ten kilograms of documents stashed away at home, which he could dig through whenever he needed to defend himself. Or to find work.

How many part-time informers' words were contained in those cellulose packages? He hadn't drawn up a precise inventory. Some of them had contributed many reports, others very few. Some were prolix, others more concise. Altogether, those *assignats* drawn on his future were worth their weight in gold.

Filip Novák had not been a first-class contributor, it has to be said. During the last two years, he had been notably less zealous in his communications: five denunciation letters, based on secondary sources; nothing terribly reprehensible in the eyes of the new authorities. The only stain on his reputation concerned his first year as an informer, when he provided the name of a courier – a Czechoslovak émigré who occasionally returned to the country to transmit messages. The man had been caught meeting the State's enemies, arrested and sentenced to eight years. He served half of that time before being expelled.

Not long after the fall of the regime, Pavel Černý realized that Bilek-Novák was doing rather well. Having sensed the wind turning, the journalist had taken care during the events of '89 to appear as a supporter of the protests. The skill with which he negotiated this bend in the road played a big part in his rapid, linear ascension thereafter; within three years, he was overseeing political and legal magazines, investigations and documentaries. Good work. Pavel Černý had thought that perhaps they could come to an understanding.

One day, feeling bold, he picked up the telephone and tried to contact him.

'I would like to speak to Mr Novák, please.'

Every time he did this, the secretary sent him packing with varying degrees of politeness. Mr Novák is not in the office, he's in a meeting, he's on holiday. After a few weeks, the detective grew weary of this. Was it time to use his silver bullet? After some hesitation, he called again, and when the secretary told him that his quest was pointless, he asked her to pass on his exact words:

'Tell him it's urgent. Ask Mr Novák to call me as soon as he can. It's about someone he used to know well: a certain Mr Bilek.'

The two men met in a café in the old town, and the hubbub around them covered up the precise terms of their verbal agreement. 'Far be it from me to try to blackmail you in any way, Mr Novák…' The detective assured him that, were the archives ever to be opened, Novák would have no cause for anxiety, for the good and simple reason that Pavel Černý would protect him: his case file was safe from prying eyes, in a secure bank vault. 'So, you see, you can sleep peacefully at night.' Of course he wasn't asking for anything in return… 'Well, just one very small thing: a bit of work.' Novák had resisted at first, pretended to be outraged: how dare you, I would never act in such a blah blah blah.

'It's one thing to have communicated certain information, Mr Bilek,' Pavel Černý said in a mildly insinuating voice. 'It's quite another to have made money from the transaction, as you did...'

'I will not allow you to say this!'

'Oh yes, you will, Mr Bilek. You most certainly will. I don't think you'd want people to start gossiping about your beautiful house, would you? Not to mention your villa, in the hills of Troja, surrounded by vines, with a roof terrace where you can get up to certain activities on summer evenings, am I right? A terrace with a view over the river and, further off, the cathedral, the Black Mountain and the White Mountain. You wouldn't want anyone to point out that your villa wasn't paid for only with your earnings as a journalist under the previous regime (which would be quite some feat), that it was funded by the prison sentences and harassment meted out to the people whose secrets you gave away... I beg your pardon: whose secrets you *sold*... Mr Bilek.'

And so, as soon as it became possible, Pavel Černý was only too happy to put his prodigious memory and secret-service know-how at the disposal of the television channel and its journalists any time that they needed information.

*

After only a year or two of staking out buildings, tailing people, and wire-tapping, Pavel Černý had proved himself the ideal freelance multipurpose factotum for public television. Novák used him with discretion and described him as his 'secret weapon'. So when Ludvík Slaný said that he needed to place Věra Foltýnova under surveillance, Filip Novák responded with a line used in many a detective story: 'I know just the man.'

In fact, Pavel Černý considered himself an expert at shadowing people. His modest apartment in Slunná even contained what he called his Shadowing Museum, which was, he boasted, the only one of its kind. This museum consisted of pairs of shoes, neatly lined up on the shelves of a storeroom. Since beginning his career, Černý had kept all the shoes he'd ever worn and had arranged them in chronological order; each pair was labelled with a pair of dates, like gravestones: the date of its arrival in his life and of its retirement. He was only half joking when he said that his memory was in his feet, that they were the repositories of a large part of his professional recollections. In the middle of the third shelf was the famous (for him, at least) pair of dark grey-green English ankle boots (1979–80), which he'd procured on the black market. A classic design. It was with deep respect that he recalled all the walking and tracking that this wonderfully supple pair of shoes had enabled him to do in those days. What an asset those boots had been in his battle against the Charter 77 people, who used to limp around in the most awful shoes... It had been a sad moment when he'd had to retire this pair, after wearing them down beyond the skills of any cobbler.

The first day he'd had to follow his prey – the only photographs of her that he'd been given were two small, grainy newspaper cuttings, showing only the woman's face, when what he needed was a shot of her back or the side of her head – the detective had tried to memorize her unremarkable physiognomy. Věra Foltýnova had very few distinguishing features and she easily melted into the crowd with her old-Czech-lady hairstyle and her Socialist-era clothing. She was so ordinary that she might have been specially designed to evade surveillance. And, while this did make Pavel uneasy, it also excited him. At last, a real challenge! He'd been asked to follow Mrs Everywoman, and that fact alone gave him hope that he was about to rediscover his love for the job. Trepidation in the face of difficulty, the unknown, the risk of failure…

That evening, the six o'clock rush on Národní had given Černý an excellent warm-up for the test to come. He had to learn by heart her bearing and her gait, although there was nothing very unique about those aspects either. The autumnal rain added an interesting difficulty: everybody was rushing forward, heads lowered, the collars of their raincoats turned up. A crowd of overcoats, trench coats and worn leather jackets came hurtling from every possible direction, from the narrow Jungmannovo Náměstí and from Na Můstku, from Václavské Náměstí and from Na Příkopě. Dozens of umbrellas opened like flowers and pushed past one another like hens in a farmyard, sometimes screening his prey from view. Luckily for him, she had gone out that evening without her umbrella. He was so tired, though, that at times he thought he was hallucinating; as if that tide of glistening caps and hats, the air around them thick with Slavic expressions, was deliberately swallowing the lady in question in order to protect her, before spitting her out in a place where the detective wasn't watching. It was almost supernatural and he couldn't believe his eyes; he didn't understand that he was just exhausted by this dense, wet crowd. In the end he lost sight of her near the entrance to the Můstek metro station, hidden in a building next to the Koruna Palace. In all likelihood the metro's mouth had swallowed her. Either that, or she'd been kidnapped by the crowd.

His first day of surveillance had not produced anything, but the game of hide-and-seek would resume the next day. Oh yes! If anyone had told him, ten years before, that ten years later he would no longer be a member of the secret police but would be reduced to playing private detective... he wouldn't have believed them and would certainly have rejected this glimpse of the future. Then again, if that same someone had added that he would be tailing a woman who claimed that Chopin was dictating posthumous compositions to her, and who had been so successful at enthusing people about these works that there would soon be a CD released, and if they'd also said that this ordinary-looking woman would spark a media frenzy, the love of mystery buried deep within him would have been awakened and he'd have thought that, all things considered, the future merited a closer look. Yes, he'd have been flattered by the idea of one day following the woman who boasted of being visited by a famous composer... A dead genius made a nice change from dissidents haunting bars into the small hours.

The first two days of surveillance did not reveal anything suspect. The back that the detective tried to keep in his sight went into food shops and made purchases; the back visited a haberdashery, an ironmonger's. Nothing out of the ordinary. Then that hypnotic back headed home. This was all Pavel Černý could pass on to Ludvík Slaný, who struck him as oddly nervous and eager.

One afternoon, walking along Národní Třída, the woman slipped into number 22 and went upstairs to sit at a café table.

He sat at another table, his back turned, but he was able to keep an eye on her in the mirror on the wall. Nobody came to sit with her. An hour passed. She leafed through a newspaper, consulted a notebook, observed a group of pool players. She probably didn't know anything about pool (nor did Černý himself), but something about the players' studied gestures and concentration seemed to captivate her. Was it their slowness? Was that their secret? It was cold outside, so the detective savoured this break, even if none of the people in the room looked anything like Chopin. The woman drank a hot chocolate with whipped cream and advocaat while he had a Fernet Stock, then a second, and he had plenty of time to get to know Mrs Everywoman's face. Even from a distance, he could tell she looked older than her late fifties; she would probably be described as a *woman of a certain age*. Yes, she looked a good ten years older than she was, probably because of that old-fashioned hairstyle. So she wasn't particularly attractive, yet Černý started to like her: she'd managed to lose him the other evening, at Můstek metro station, and that was not something that many people could do. First he had been annoyed with her, and then he'd been annoyed with himself. Gradually, however, after suffering this blow to his self-esteem, he had forgiven her. She interested him. Just like a hunter loves the animals that he tracks through the undergrowth, a detective always feels great respect for his prey. It was a curious relationship, the watcher and the watched. He'd been hypnotized by the back of his prey. He'd taken the bait and now he was hooked. There was a connection between them. He was ready to follow her wherever she led him, not because he needed to earn money, but because an invisible line ran from his mouth to her fishing rod.

Nobody came to meet her. It was just her and her cup of hot chocolate. A shame. Unless she'd been summoned there by a dead man and she was communicating with him in sips? He never took his eyes off her reflection in the large wall mirror. Occasionally, however, he would catch a glimpse of his own face and wonder how well he really blended into the background of this posh *kavárna*. He usually went unnoticed, with his average height, his chestnut hair and his features so unremarkable that people often couldn't remember whether or not he'd been at a meeting. All this helped to make him the 'perfect shadow', except for a few nervous tics. These tics had afflicted him in adolescence and then disappeared, but his divorce the previous year had brought them back. The more he tried to suppress them, the more insistently they taunted him, and Černý couldn't help fearing that one day they would betray him.

*

The next morning, he parked his blue-green Skoda 100 (nobody, not even the car salesman, had been able to tell him whether it was actually blue or green) near the woman's apartment building. He'd made a thermos of coffee in anticipation of a prolonged siege: the temperature had dropped almost to zero the night before, and it was now November so he didn't expect the weather to improve any time soon.

Nine o'clock... nine-thirty... nine-forty. He was starting to get used to the idea of a whole morning stuck in his car, breathing in the odour of his Sparta cigarettes, when she appeared in the doorway. This time, she hadn't forgotten her umbrella. He got out of the car and followed her at a distance. Would she take the tram? The metro? It was the morning of All Saints' Day and he feared that she was headed to the cemetery. He wasn't wrong, but he also wasn't quite imaginative enough to see what that might mean.

From Jugoslávská, she walked up to Náměstí Míru, where she caught the metro; a moment later, she got out at Flora and he understood. After buying a bunch of heather, she walked resolutely along the paths of the vast cemetery. He did the same, behind her, not waiting for his change after he'd paid because he didn't want to lose her. A few minutes later, she put the heather on a stone slab engraved with the image of a serious-looking man: JAN FOLTYN 1938–1984. Her husband hadn't lasted long… Half hidden behind a tree, Pavel Černý observed the widow through his Zeiss binoculars. After cleaning off the slab, she took several glasses containing white candles from her bag and placed them at the corners of the tomb, then lit them with a lighter. She delicately closed the metal lid of each one and gathered her thoughts. After that, she picked up an old pot of flowers and tossed it in a rubbish bin. But the detective was intrigued. She had a second plastic bag… and he could see other candles inside it.

Věra Foltýnova walked back towards the metro, but instead of going back to Náměstí Míru, she changed at Můstek and took the B train to Karlovo Náměstí. Hmm, thought Černý, leaving the rest of his thoughts in suspense and following her along the Rašín embankment.

The leaden sky that he'd noticed in the distance when he left Olšany was now showering them with enormous raindrops. Then a storm broke and hailstones began lashing the pavement. He tried not to lose sight of her amid the sudden flowering of black umbrellas. Everything went fine until she turned onto Vnislavova, after the railway bridge. A few moments later, just after entering Libušina, she vanished. 'Damn it, I lost her!' cursed the detective. She was going to escape him again. The street was curved; he glanced towards Vratislavova and thought he saw her. *Was* that her? A gust of wind turned the woman's umbrella inside out and he saw that he'd been right. It wasn't the first time she'd briefly vanished from sight that day, since leaving her apartment; each time he lost her like that, he started sweating, despite all his experience of shadowing people from a distance, and he couldn't relax until she'd reappeared in his field of vision.

Now she'd gone into a food shop, which gave him a brief respite. He lit a cigarette. The journalist had asked him to stay in touch whenever he could, throughout the day, and he spotted a telephone booth on the other side of the street.

It rang twice before the journalist answered.

'Ludvík Slaný?'

The scream of a siren drowned out his voice for a few seconds.

'IT'S ME, ČERNÝ!' he yelled. 'She's just gone into a shop so I've got a minute to talk to you. She's a fast walker, your client, it's not easy to follow her with all these crowds... Yes... This morning, she left home just before ten and went to Olšany to leave flowers on her husband's grave... Yes, just the one. Nothing special... Actually, I did notice one thing that struck me as odd:

she put a pot of flowers down, swept away the dead leaves, and then she just stood there for a while. Like someone gathering their thoughts, you know… I don't know how else to put it.'

'What's strange about that? It was her husband's grave.'

'Yes. But she did say Chopin wasn't the only person who appeared to her, right? That dead people have been visiting her ever since she was a child? So don't you find it weird that she stood for several minutes in front of that grave when she maybe just "saw" her husband the day before or even that morning, at home, and "had a discussion" with him? Putting flowers on his grave is one thing, but hanging around afterwards…'

This remark plunged Ludvík into a state of deep perplexity.

'Well, she couldn't just put the flowers there and leave, could she?'

'Before standing there, doing nothing, she'd already spent five minutes cleaning the slab, scraping off moss, and so on.'

'How long did she spend gathering her thoughts?'

'I didn't time it, but at least ten minutes… What? TEN! Then she took the metro… THE METRO! And she got out at Karlovo Náměstí and… Shit, here she comes again… I said HERE SHE COMES! It's just as I thought, she's going towards… I'm going to hang up. I'll call you back when I can.'

Černý continued along V Pevnosti then entered the castle through the Cihelná Brána. Now he understood the reason for the second bag. The woman climbed the steps, walked beside an outer wall and went into the cemetery. Who could she know that was resting in here? He let her move sixty feet ahead; despite the fact that it was All Saints' Day, there were very few people here. He passed Slavín and saw her near the arcade gallery, where she stopped. Without letting her out of his sight, he moved a little closer, sheltered by the gravestones and trees, the ivy, the stone crosses; he pretended to be searching for some famous name. What was she doing over there? Whose grave could it be? When he was sure he'd identified the tomb she was standing before, he froze. The sound of distant car horns was carried to his ears by the wind.

This inseparable couple paused again in their strange dance across the city. The man was in his forties, wearing a dark raincoat, half hidden by a forest of crosses, and the woman in her fifties, edging dangerously close to her sixties, with her rigidly set hair.

The woman in the grey coat stood for a few minutes in front of the tomb and then walked away. The detective carefully approached, fearing that she might return for some reason, but no: she was heading resolutely towards the security gate.

Sepulchre number 38, before which Věra Foltýnova had stood, was considerably older and less well kept than its neighbours. It lay at the base of a tree whose trunk had split. She'd swept it but hadn't attempted to pull the weeds from its edges. There was quite a bit of moss on the slab; time had left its patina there. Mrs Foltýnova had lit a candle and the flame was flickering under its metal lid. It was a spartan tomb. No photograph printed on a ceramic plaque, as on the other graves. The person buried in this particular spot had no face.

Suddenly, belatedly understanding the strangeness of what he was looking at, the detective gasped, his hand to his mouth. Instinctively, he turned towards the end of the path, half-expecting the woman to be gloating over his surprise from a distance, laughing to herself, but she had gone. She was already walking her mysterious route again. The pale sun reappeared between clouds and Pavel Černý nervously took a Polaroid camera from his bag. He carefully framed the picture, then pressed the button. It wouldn't be a very good photograph, but that hardly mattered.

VIII

'IN 1995, DANA, back when Novák commissioned me to make that documentary, there was no such thing as email or the World Wide Web, and that made my task a lot simpler. After the first interviews with Věra Foltýnova, I came to the conclusion that this woman had created a perfect system and that only some good old-fashioned espionage would enable us to see through it. I wanted to know who she was mixing with. Among the living, I mean. Novák was of the same opinion as me: a woman from such a modest background who played the piano like a removal man couldn't possibly be operating without some hidden accomplice. Chopin's music is so complex, it was unthinkable that she could imitate it at all, never mind produce hundreds of pieces. No, this Foltýnova woman had to be the figurehead of a masterful artistic swindle, and I fully intended to expose it. From then on, my investigation became a sort of treasure hunt. Novák was prepared to give me the time and resources I needed because, he said, we had to do the exact opposite of what all the other media had done: repeating the woman's claims without verifying them, merely skimming the surface instead of diving more deeply. Anything we stated, we would first have to prove. I liked his plan and was happy to go along with it because this was, at last, an opportunity to do my job the way I'd always dreamt of doing it: leaving no stone unturned in the search for truth.

'Yes, Novák and I were on the same wavelength. Was this down to the steadying influence of Roman, who was always a good judge and who'd won me over to his way of seeing things? Novák appeared sincere to me, and soon I had no more doubts about him. He gave me free rein and didn't interfere. I realized that my initial fears that he was laying a trap for me had been unfounded. In truth, he would have liked to make that documentary himself, but he had a whole channel to run and he wasn't the sort of person who could delegate such tasks for a few weeks while he followed his heart. What he'd given me was not a poisoned chalice, it was a gift horse, and I wasn't about to look it in the mouth. So… enough with the paranoia! None of this had anything to do with Zdeňka. In a way, I was acting as Novák's proxy: he was trusting me and guiding me where he wanted me to go. I think he knew me much better than I'd realized, and that was why he chose me. My scientific mind, which he'd gone on and on about, was just a pretext… I was a puppet and he was pulling the strings.

'Novák and I had thought about the best way to monitor our supposed medium. Reading her letters. Bugging her phone. Following her visitors. Following *her.* But who knew what other modes of communication she might be using that hadn't occurred to us? Anyone who could compose such brilliant pastiches had to be an expert in fraud.

'We were in the protohistoric part of the information age back then. The new technologies were still in their early stages and we had to use traditional methods to outwit our impostor. We couldn't spy on her emails, for example... How old were you, Dana, when Czechoslovakia split in two? All of that seems so distant to me now. Twenty years... It was a strange time. We were all still in shock, I think, caught between euphoria and bafflement, astounded to wake up one fine morning in two countries when we had gone to sleep the night before in one. The country had been sliced in half not long before, like a single-cell organism reproducing with binary fission, isolating the Czechs on one side and the Slovaks on the other. Regrets were already festering. And it was exactly at that moment that I had to get into a fight with Mrs Foltýnova and her messengers from beyond the grave... I knew almost nothing about her, but the woman I met was a dinner lady who had no musical ear. My curiosity was piqued: it was such an obvious casting error on Chopin's part. That just made the whole story even more intriguing.

'Novák gave me carte blanche to carry out a surveillance operation worthy of the Cold War: she was staked out, tailed... But I knew that wouldn't be enough in itself. I was prepared to do anything. I could always call on Novák's support if I ran into any legal difficulties. According to him, there was no problem intercepting her phone calls: we just had to ask the intelligence service – they would willingly do us a favour in return for the information that we fed them occasionally. And then there was her post. "Don't forget her letters," Novák said, getting into the spirit of things. "They're bound to help us get a better idea what's going on."

'The big advantage that I had over you, Dana, was being able to operate in a period of flux. Greasing palms was common currency back then, a survival reflex in every section of society. The methods of the communist era hadn't given way to the new methods yet. I had more room for manoeuvre than you will have. You'll have to follow the rules, respect individual privacy, abide by the letter of the law. You can't bribe administrators or policemen anymore to make them turn a blind eye to what you're up to…

'Now I think about it, I made that documentary at the ideal time. Ten years earlier, it wouldn't have been possible at all, for obvious reasons, and ten years later, everything would have been so much more difficult. I'm not trying to discourage you, Dana. You're going into battle with all the optimism of youth; you believe in this crazy profession more than I do, and that's to your credit. I must warn you of one thing, however. If you show an interest in this woman, you'll come to realize that she's isolated from us by an invisible screen. You'll remember me telling you that this affair was my most successful failure. You're young: words don't have exactly the same weight or meaning for you and for me, either side of this table which has heard so many conversations before ours. The beer is loosening my tongue. What I'm telling you about tonight is the most fulfilling failure I've had since starting out in this job; the most fulfilling and the most self-enlightening since I started rummaging through the lives of others. I'm not talking about a failure for my ego – that's something else entirely. I'm talking about this documentary, which was a Herculean task, even if I did manage to finish it in the end, in circumstances that I'll explain to you.

I'm talking about the part of oneself that grows only in times of crisis, with the fear of falling into the abyss.

'Roman thought I was seeing the devil everywhere I looked. That Novák and I were getting all worked up over nothing. "Just look at things simply," he kept advising me, but I didn't really grasp the meaning of that word *simply*. "You're creating a conspiracy theory, but there is no conspiracy," he insisted. Oh, he was careful not to antagonize me, because he knew perfectly well that I was headed in a precise direction and I wasn't going to change my mind. "So what you believe," I said to him sarcastically, "is that Chopin comes to visit her at teatime every day? And, after nibbling a few biscuits, he dictates his latest compositions to her? Is that right?"

'My cameraman's reply was evasive: "That's not what I meant. Don't take it the wrong way. And don't twist my words."

'"I'm simply trying to understand you, since you keep talking about simplicity."

'"All I'm saying is that there might be a third way, between the huge swindle that you imagine and visits from beyond the grave. There are other possibilities, don't you think?"'

'Like what?' (It was Dana, excited, who asked this question.)

'Dana, it took me a long time to broaden the field of the acceptable. A long time, some terrible moments, the questioning of everything I thought I knew... It's strange how far the mind can bend if you put it under enough pressure. That's what happens as you get older: your body stiffens as your mind grows more supple. "Like what?" you ask. I fear you'll have to spend a long time listening to me, and you'll have to drink quite a few more beers, before you have a clear idea of what happened.

You'll discover what I now believe to be, not the absolute truth, but the beginning of an explanation. You'll learn what doesn't appear in my documentary; everything I kept to myself. Your smile is inviting me to keep talking. And, since I like your smile, since I find it compelling, I'm going to do what you wish.'

IX

THAT MORNING, Ludvík wanted to show the cameraman the photograph from the cemetery before they went to see Věra Foltýnova, but Roman had told him that he wasn't going to make the meeting on time and had asked Ludvík to prepare for the shoot without him. He was sorry, but he would only be twenty minutes late. Half an hour, at most.

The photograph continued to trouble Ludvík. With his fingertips, he felt its presence in his pocket. During his 3.15 a.m. insomnia (for months now, he had mysteriously been waking up at that precise time – the Achilles heel of an insomniac's night – and not being able to fall back asleep until five or six), he'd kept turning over the possibility of showing it to Věra Foltýnova, with no warning whatsoever, while the camera recorded her reaction, monitored her face for the slightest sign of emotion. Was he going to do it? It would certainly provide him with what those in the business called 'a nice shot', but – at the same time – it would lift the veil on their surveillance of her, and it was far too early for that. Oh well... another time, perhaps? Unless he found some explanation of the mystery before then.

No, the surprise that Ludvík had in mind for Chopin's secretary, that day, was something else completely. He'd thought about it vaguely during their first meeting and the idea had resurfaced thanks to his latest bout of insomnia, which had given him time to think it through. The idea was seductive. He was going to catch her off guard, ruffle the feathers of this remarkably placid woman. And he was also going to catch his cameraman off guard – his way of paying Roman back for being late and reminding him who was boss. It was risky, but he would abide by all the rules, take all possible precautions to ensure she didn't clam up or guess that he was luring her into a trap.

It had been agreed that, if she entered into communication with Chopin that day, she would note down what he dictated to her while the camera was rolling. She would transcribe the tune in accordance with the method she said she'd adopted with him: in pencil, on music paper, without playing it first.

That was how the meeting should go. It was in her interests, after all, to convince them that she was in communication with the composer, thought Ludvík, feeling certain that she would play her role with great flair.

His intuition wasn't wrong. Half an hour after Roman's arrival, while they were continuing the interview begun during the second meeting, she suddenly said:

'He's here.'

'You see him?'

'Very clearly. Sometimes the communication isn't good, but that's not the case today. I have a perfect view of him. I'm going to suggest that he gives me a composition.'

'Before that, I have a request for you. For both of you.'

The moment had come, Ludvík decided. Time to play his trump card. Asking Roman to turn the camera towards him, he pointed at the portraits of the children and the late husband which adorned the living-room walls.

'Věra Foltýnova, we have already noted your highly developed artistic sense. The portraits we can admire in this room are testimony to that. And since, at this moment, you tell us that Chopin is with you and that you can see him very clearly, I would like to suggest a little experiment that will help to prove your good faith to anyone who has doubts. If your visitor agrees and is willing to show a little patience, would you please draw him as you see him this morning?'

The cameraman looked stupefied. Věra Foltýnova, on the other hand, kept calm. She made a plausible excuse: 'I'm afraid I don't draw anymore. I've done nothing in recent years, and I fear I must be very rusty. Besides, I don't even have any pencils or...'

'I brought along everything you'll need,' interrupted Ludvík, taking the materials from his bag. 'Please, take your time. As I said, this is just to demonstrate your good faith...'

'All right,' she said after a few seconds of silence. 'But I can't make any guarantees. I've only ever drawn from photographs, which gives me as long as I need. I've never asked anyone to keep still before...'

Your model has all the time in the world, Ludvík thought but didn't say.

She'd been forced to agree and he was pleased with his trap. If Roman had objected, Ludvík would have put him in his place, but, as it was, the cameraman said nothing.

The experiment could begin.

Ludvík was intrigued by the blank space in the doorway that Mrs Foltýnova stared at, as if to make them believe that her model was standing there, where he himself detected no presence at all. Věra's eyes flickered back and forth between the sheet of paper and that blank space, and the journalist thought: she's a brilliant liar. He observed her left hand as it made marks on the page, and then her eyes as they looked up at the space, which he estimated to be about five feet and three inches above the floor. He found himself thinking that he'd have to check the biographies to find out the composer's height, and then he grew irritated with himself: he was inadvertently playing by his opponent's rules, giving unnecessary credence to her deception. He was angry that he'd lost control of his thoughts, even for a moment. But then his anger faded and he watched excitedly as she rubbed something out, hesitated. She didn't look too confident now, he thought. Presumably she was trying to remember the portraits of Chopin by Delacroix or Kolberg to help her out of this fix. Was she cursing him? He would have given anything to overhear her thoughts at that moment.

Cornered like this, would she make some specious excuse and abandon the experiment? Say that she couldn't concentrate for that long, that the communication was becoming less clear? She might argue that the outlines of the apparition were growing too vague to draw with any precision, like a radio station fading in and out. She could say that it was getting too difficult, that Chopin was hidden, his features veiled by a sort of mist…

But Věra said nothing. She kept her eyes fixed on the same blank space and the minutes ticked by. Ludvík could hear the faint scrape of pencil on paper.

She was concentrating hard. Ludvík Slaný hadn't imagined that she would last this long. From the chair where he sat (he didn't dare get up, for fear of disturbing her focus and being blamed for ruining the experiment), he couldn't see what was forming on the sheet of paper, he could only listen – in a religious silence – to that *scrape-scrape-scrape*, like the sound of an insect's footsteps or the needle of a seismograph. The only thing he could see changing was the woman's face: furrowed brow, creased forehead, narrowed eyes… and then the expressions that moved furtively over her features, like a cloud above a wheat field: weariness, discouragement, even flickers of distress. What a remarkable actress she is, Ludvík observed, who only then noticed the smell of lilac in the apartment.

After a while, she broke the silence: she was going to focus on his face and just rough out the rest – hair, ears, scarf around his neck – if that was all right? Ludvík gave his consent with a slight movement of his chin. He didn't want to interrupt her defeat. Let her sink! Let the blank page suck her down like quicksand. He could read the nervousness on the woman's puckered forehead, as if her fears were plainly written there in deep, shadowy lines. Still, she kept going, and she seemed to rediscover the degree of concentration she'd had at the beginning, as if refreshed by a new wave of energy. From time to time, something flashed in her eyes. Long minutes of concentration followed, and then – without turning towards them – she said:

'I think I've captured his expression. The eyes are always the most difficult part… the eyes and the lips. Once you've got those, everything else comes easily. See for yourself… What do you think?'

She showed them the sheet of paper, forgetting that the camera was still rolling. Ludvík Slaný shuddered when he saw the fragments of that face materializing on the page. Not only was this woman a great actress but she had not lost her ability to draw. He couldn't tell if the eyes were really Chopin's, but they were certainly somebody's, not the mere product of her imagination, scribbled onto paper to fool them. When she started drawing again, the journalist's mood was somewhat altered. There was an ominous feeling in his chest. For the moment, all she'd done was 'preface' Chopin. The eyes, the sides of his nose… And now, she said, she was going to draw his mouth.

Things didn't take long after that, as if – after she had captured the expression in his eyes (or so she said) – the rest simply surrendered. What she wrested from that blank space gradually appeared on paper, like a photograph forming in a developing bath. After finishing the lips, the artist delineated the corners of the eyes and perfected the outline of the nose, then she sketched in his hair and ears, his neck, her pencil strokes more casual now. She was smiling when she handed Ludvík the sheet of paper. He felt his right hand tighten around the Polaroid at the bottom of his pocket. He was ready to brandish it as evidence, but at the last moment he held back. The dish of vengeance had to cool a little first.

Only a curmudgeon could have failed to acknowledge that the face on the paper genuinely resembled Chopin. The calm humility in his eyes. The telltale bump on his nose. Roman Staněk gasped. And to crown it all, the patiently drawn Chopin wore a lightly mocking expression.

Quick, break this awkward silence! Ludvík was dumbstruck, but he needed to say something to rid himself of an unpleasant feeling.

'Chopin looks quite young in your picture...'

'Yes, I would say about twenty-seven or twenty-eight, wouldn't you? It's from before his illness, in any case...'

'Before his troubles in Majorca.'

'Yes. So probably about 1836 or 1837.'

'And that's how he appears to you? Does he always look the same? And how does he behave towards you?'

'Yes, he always looks like that. With handsome blue eyes. As for his attitude, I would sum it up in two words: elegance and courtesy. From time to time, I can sense that he would like me to understand him and to write more quickly. But it's not something we can change: I can't go faster than the music... He never loses patience, never raises his voice. We sometimes laugh at my carelessness. In fact, we laugh quite a lot, about everyday things. We don't talk about music... Was he like that when he was alive? The Chopin who visits me is not anxious or depressed. Just a romantic with a melancholic nature. I was a little surprised by that to start with. Perplexed.'

She was tired out by the drawing, so they decided to postpone the film of her taking dictation of a composition until the next day. Down in the street, Ludvík walked beside his cameraman and said in a low voice: 'How can anyone have such perfect recall as to be able to reproduce a face in such detail? I'm impressed by her memory, I must admit. What about you?'

'Her memory? What's that got to do with it?'

Ludvík felt suddenly alone. Roman was good at his job, of course, but when it came to this particular subject, they were not on the same wavelength at all, which was annoying. How could he be so mesmerized by Věra Foltýnova, Ludvík wondered. The cameraman's critical faculties had been altered, he thought. He no longer had the distance necessary for a journalist to be *objective* about his subject. Probably because he didn't feel he was getting the support he needed, Ludvík took the photograph from his pocket and showed it to Roman.

'What's that?'

'On All Saints' Day, after visiting her husband's grave in Olšany, she went to another cemetery where she paid her respects at this gravestone. Černý took this picture, but he couldn't shed any further light on it.'

'There's no name on that gravestone!'

'Exactly. And Černý is certain that there's no mistake. She stayed there for a moment to gather her thoughts and sweep away a few dead leaves. The grave is close to a row of arches; it won't be difficult to find.'

'This is in Vyšehrad?'

'Yes.'

'And you didn't ask her for an explanation?'

'Who, Foltýnova?'

'Yes.'

'So she'd know she was being tailed? Let's just let the detective do his job first. You see? He's already started providing us with some interesting information.'

X

AND WE TURN the pages of our days without savouring their unique flavour. These little treasures escape us before we have time to catch our breath. No sooner have we skimmed through those pages than we want to know what happened next. Insatiably we turn to the next chapter, entitled 'winter' or 'summer' or 'spring' or 'autumn', and then we're already on the next part: 'the new year'. Whole pages and chapters swallowed up to the rhythm of waltzes or mazurkas, or a prelude hinting at unexpected developments... These melodies entertain us like the orchestra on the *Titanic* kept its passengers distracted from their doom. It's good to take your mind off things while you wait for the funeral march.

The day after Chopin appeared on a sheet of drawing paper, Ludvík Slaný and his cameraman went back to Mrs Foltýnova's apartment, accompanied by a sound technician, in the hope of filming her while she took dictation of a composition. Had she learnt one of the works by heart so she'd be able to pretend to hear it directly from the dead man? When he saw the sound equipment, the lights and the camera, Ludvík had a sudden urge to laugh. What a merry dance she was leading them, all these rational, scientific men! How easily they were dazzled by her sleight of hand: pulling Chopin from her hat instead of a rabbit! Look at that piano… It looks completely normal, doesn't it? And yet, in five minutes, it will play you a brand new mazurka that you'll love!

When all the equipment had been installed and they began to wait in silence, Ludvík felt like a trapper watching his snare. But the animal he was trying to catch was, he knew, particularly cunning. Schadenfreude: there's no real equivalent for this word in Czech, so it would have to be translated, in that moment, as 'the joy of seeing Věra Foltýnova fall flat on her face', or as 'pleasure at the idea that she will vanish into oblivion after being unmasked'… Either way, that was the word that came to Ludvík's mind when he saw her look flustered.

After a certain amount of time, he was expecting her to claim that she couldn't enter into communication with the great man and to suggest that they try again another time, when the celestial scrambling devices had been unplugged. If the surveillance operations bore fruit, if he ended up uncovering the scam, he would be able to say in the voiceover, at this point in the documentary: 'Here is Mrs Foltýnova pretending to wait for a messenger from the other side of the border – the most secure border of all, next to which the Berlin Wall was little more than a pile of bricks.' Such was Ludvík's intention, but he could sense that something else was hatching inside him, something that as yet had no name: a sort of newfound curiosity that his mind had never conceived before. He was like a little boy who goes to the toilets at school and, for the first time, puts his eye to the hole in the dividing wall.

She had warned them: with all the activity of a film crew in the room, she couldn't promise anything. And yet they didn't have long to wait. After five minutes, she moved from her chair to the piano stool, and there, leaning down and holding the notebook against the music stand with her left hand, she started to write on the blank sheet music. She was fully focused on what she was doing, her eyes fixed to the staves. All those notes, thought Ludvík: round and tiny, attaching themselves to the black lines like swallows on electric wires. 'A scherzo,' she announced. 'I asked him if he had something bright and lively for us today...' She traced the minims, crotchets and quavers in pencil, and sometimes, when she'd misunderstood something, she would erase those little graphite flakes. 'I asked him if he could supply us with a few clues that would allow you to prove that the composition was really by him. Little markers that might convince the musicologists...'

It was clear from the way she counted the lines that she was far from self-assured. Sometimes, the pencil end would hesitate, hovering a few millimetres above the paper, and then the gentle scraping sound would resume. Ludvík and Roman held their breath, afraid that a single cough or throat-clearing could cause a disturbance. What was at stake here, thought Ludvík, was the issue of posterity: this apocryphal Chopin would only gain widespread public approval if he could manage to persuade people that it was by the *actual* Chopin. Ludvík couldn't wait to hear how it would sound. The piece currently being transcribed was a fake banknote bearing the composer's effigy. Now the question remained: was the forger a genius? Soon, he thought eagerly, soon he would be able to listen to these notes, to submit them to experts.

Věra traced the notes, the quavers' tails and the lines connecting them without even pausing. Ludvík was astonished by the regularity of her rhythm. Sometimes the dots that she sowed climbed to the octave above, and sometimes they tumbled down. Occasionally she would comment on what she was doing while continuing to write, as if she could function with part of her mind in this world and another part in that world. At times, she talked to herself: 'Ah yes… That's right…' And she murmured notes: 'Sol… re…' First she would record five or six bars for the left hand, and then the same for the right. Despite her fierce focus, she never lost her cheerful tone: 'I can't believe that's right…' She played two or three bars then, before quietly concluding: 'No, that's good… Sometimes what I write down seems a bit strange, you know?… But that's it… It's easy to make a mistake…'

About forty-five minutes had passed when she turned to them with an apologetic look. 'He's not there anymore. It's annoying when you lose contact like that… I'm probably a bit tense.'

She didn't seem upset. This sort of thing must happen all the time: a fuse blows, you replace it, and the light comes back on. She relaxed, gazing at the keyboard, and did nothing for a few seconds. Then, in a calmer voice: 'It's all right, I can still see him. It's better when I sit like this.'

For some time now, Ludvík had felt a vague, nagging sense of unease. The word *discrepancy* floated through his thoughts, although he couldn't work out how to use it in a logical sentence. Perhaps a certain discrepancy between what he'd imagined and what he was observing. Watching this scene, watching her, it struck him that it probably came from the fact that she was wholly absorbed in what she was doing. Deep down, although he didn't want to admit it, everything he'd seen of her led him to believe that she wasn't faking at all.

A little later, she told them, in an amused tone: 'Hmm, he's asking me to speed up… I can't go any faster than this…' And she continued writing.

About an hour after the meeting had begun, she announced: 'The piece isn't finished. It became too difficult. I was finding it harder and harder to hear him properly and I didn't want to make any mistakes.' She sounded sorry, but no more than that. 'He told me that we have about half of it. We can finish it in the next few days. What's here probably corresponds to about four or five minutes…'

She thought there might be a couple of bars missing, but she didn't seem very worried about it. Chopin had told her as the meeting ended that he'd given her thirty-two bars, but when she counted them up she found only thirty. 'Two of them must have got lost in the communication. I'll have to ask him about that.'

Nobody asked her to, but she felt an urge to play the whole piece and she started without too much difficulty, after reminding them that she wasn't an experienced pianist. She was so focused on the music that she seemed to forget about the camera. What she'd transcribed must have been particularly tough because she suddenly stopped after a few bars.

'Sorry. I just can't seem to concentrate properly today. I'll have to practise…'

'Would you mind?' The sound technician, who had been silent until now, walked towards the piano. 'I don't play very often these days, but I've always loved deciphering a new score… May I?'

The notes, those swallows on electrical wires, were waiting for the signal to become sounds and take flight. Ludvík could have sworn that his cameraman had fallen into the same state as him. It was a state difficult to define – midway between astonishment and admiration – but he felt utterly captive to it. Why hide how beautiful he found this music? It was so far removed from a simple, unimaginative copy of Chopin that Ludvík turned pale as he listened. When it was over, Roman asked him if he was all right and he replied that he had no idea their sound engineer was so talented. Then he thanked the sound man for allowing them to hear this… this… At that point in the sentence he just stammered because he couldn't think how to describe what he'd just heard.

*

The entrance hall of 57 Londýnská was long and dark: perfect, thought Pavel Černý, when he first saw it. The wall was covered with letterboxes, and the postman came here to deliver letters at exactly nine-forty every morning. A few minutes later, he exited the building and continued on to the next one, as if this was all he'd ever done since the dawn of time.

Černý usually began his day by emptying Mrs Foltýnova's letterbox as soon as the postman had left; he dived into the corridor and, without triggering the motion sensor, used either his hand (his fingers were long and slender, like a pianist's hands, according to his mother) or a pair of pliers or a wire with glue on the end to harpoon and remove that morning's post. Černý knew all the tricks of the trade, and it never took him more than a few seconds to complete this operation. Naturally, he had a ready-made excuse in case anyone happened to catch him: he always carried a pile of advertising leaflets, so at worst he could be accused of filling people's letterboxes with junk.

It was rare that his mission was interrupted. But it did happen one sunny morning when the door of the entrance hall opened to reveal the silhouettes of two men standing in the doorway. Černý felt a sudden surge of adrenaline, then the hallway light came on and he recognized the television journalist – the man who had commissioned him to do this work – accompanied by a cameraman. He winked at them and left: they never talked when they were on a job, and of course he couldn't follow them up to the woman's apartment. There, Ludvík asked about the ghost's curiosity. Was Chopin (he'd decided to call him that, partly for the sake of convenience and partly to win over the medium, but he always did it reluctantly) curious about the reception of his works in the modern world? Did he sometimes give her his opinion about the way they were played?

Just as this question was being asked, Pavel Černý was going home to steam open the woman's letters, study their contents, then reseal the envelopes. The next day, after stealing that morning's post, he would drop the previous day's letters into the letterbox.

Three floors above him, Ludvík was thinking that perhaps one of the letters that the detective had taken would contain sheet music sent to her by some unknown person, and this idea reassured him. He continued interviewing the imperturbable Věra Foltýnova and her sincerity continued to confound him… but he who laughs last laughs longest, he reminded himself. He would force her into a mistake. And he repeated to himself the words that, during difficult moments in his life, had helped him so much that they'd become a sort of motto: 'Victory goes to he who suffers fifteen minutes longer than his enemy.' The phrase wasn't his. It was attributed to General Nogi, a famous Japanese strategist who drove the Russians to surrender at Port Arthur after a long siege. Just fifteen minutes longer than the strange Mrs Foltýnova, with her natural charm, thought poor General Ludvík. For now, she didn't even seem to be suffering…

The journalist listened as she told him what Chopin thought of his best interpreters: Samson François, Horowitz, Argerich, Pogorelich. This will be excellent for the documentary, he thought delightedly, drinking in her words. Music aficionados will be desperate to see this. 'A violinist,' Ludvík said, 'originally from Hungary, who – like you – was a gifted medium, summoned the spirit of Robert Schumann with a Ouija board and asked him questions about the best way to interpret some of his works. When you're dictating music by Chopin, do you sometimes ask that kind of thing, as the violinist did?'

'You know, I try very hard to transcribe everything he tells me as best I can. If I make a mistake, he corrects me; sometimes I get flustered, the communication falters, and that's it for the day… I do my best to stay focused but, as I told you, I had no musical training. I often feel helpless. But I tell myself that the reason Chopin chose me – instead of someone more competent, like your Hungarian violinist – was *because I know nothing.* Don't you think? I can't add any personal touch to the music. I'm never tempted to alter it, edit it… there's no discussion, in other words. So no, I don't ask him any questions of that sort.'

'Interesting… So he needed a perfect Philistine.'

'I feel sure that's what he had in mind. Why else would he choose a silly old goose like me?'

She smiled mischievously. She obviously believes what she's saying, Ludvík thought once again. So… what if she wasn't a good actress? What if she was genuinely convinced by everything she claimed? He found this theory both irritating and strangely seductive.

The three men left her apartment and walked slowly, dreamily towards the sound technician's car. They were about to go their separate ways when the sound engineer said: 'I don't believe stuff like that. But when I started playing the score that she'd written down, I believed in Chopin's work.'

All three of them looked serious and Roman tried to lighten the mood. 'All we need now is the machine that Prospero Lapagese was trying to develop… You haven't heard of it? It'd be perfect for us right now… His device was supposed to record the voices of spirits and to photograph them too. And if that didn't work, we could always try George Meek's Spiricom…'

'Well, Mr Spirit, if you want to start directing this documentary and swallowing everything the old bat says, then go ahead… Take my place!'

Ludvík hated giving way to anger like this, and he immediately regretted his words. It only happened when he felt overwhelmed, when his anxiety – like a pressure cooker – threatened to explode.

*

Until now, the letterbox had not revealed anything suspect whatsoever. Thanks to the incestuous relationship between the intelligence services and the press, and to the somewhat blurred legal status of such activities, Věra Foltýnova's telephone was now being tapped. The surveillance operation was in full swing and, every morning, Pavel waited inside his car for the woman to come out so he could follow her. He knew all her favourite shops and could have made most of her daily walk with his eyes closed: along the Masaryk embankment, or sometimes – on the other side of the river – the Jánaček embankment; after that, she would wander through back streets on the Left Bank and then enter Petřín, where she would stroll more slowly before emerging above the Lobkowicz Palace. She seemed indifferent to the cold and the rain, and on sunny days this solar-powered pedestrian would walk even further and faster, as if her intention was to exhaust poor Černý, who cursed her.

She was a loner and a home bird. This was good news for her pursuers, who at least never had to leave the city or take a taxi. She almost always walked everywhere, only taking public transport for journeys to the most distant parts of town.

She was a loner, but not always. She had two friends, whom she would meet in a café in the city centre, sometimes just one of them, sometimes both. She would regularly meet one of them at the Lucerna, for endless games of chess. The two women would sit at a table near the alcove, above the covered passageway, while Černý leant on the bar, a dark and monstrous thing like the prow of a ship splitting the room in two. The detective never took off his black leather jacket, as if he didn't plan to stay there long, and lost himself in the pages of *Lidové noviny*, which he pretended to read from front to back while in reality he watched his prey in the large mirror opposite him. Sometimes there would be a rush of voices coming down the stairs that led from the cinema next door: a film had just ended and they were all discussing it. The detective gritted his teeth. Another lost day. This woman was leading him by the nose, always several steps ahead of him. She probably had dozens of works by 'Chopin' lying in drawers around her apartment, enough to sustain a long siege. But in that case, what was the point of this surveillance? Černý's back and bottom were aching from the hours spent on bar stools. Sometimes he would slip away as a group of cinemagoers descended the stairs and walk towards Vodičkova or Štěpánská while, at the women's table, a pawn or a knight were finally taken after intense cogitation.

How many afternoons had Pavel Černý spent at the bar, or at a distant table, near the piano or the door? He had too much time to think, and his thoughts were as untimely as they were absurd. They went off in his head like grenades. Stop, Pavel, he told himself, calm down. This is a new era and you're not living in a spy novel. One day, he started to feel sure that the movement of pawns by Mrs Foltýnova's opponent was a sort of code for communicating the notes of a new waltz. Stop it, he reminded himself, you're not making any sense! These women aren't stealing the plans for a missile base. If her friend had a score to give her, she'd just hand it over in an envelope or slip it into her bag. At one point the detective told himself: this woman is driving you crazy; she's succeeding where all the old State enemies failed.

One evening, after 'accompanying' her to her street, he felt convinced that she wouldn't be going out again that night. But he still got in his car and waited, in the cold air, for the lights to come on behind the third-floor windows. Only then did he give himself permission to start the engine. He had a long journey ahead of him: through the rush-hour traffic to his apartment building near Říčany, and he sighed with relief as he turned the key in the lock. He was desperate for a bath. He turned the key once, twice, three times, and still the engine didn't growl. No sound at all. 'Shit!' he hissed. What a thing to happen on an evening like this, the streets covered in melting snow, and it was already past seven o'clock! He really couldn't imagine taking public transport, but he had no idea whose bell he could ring in search of a place to spend the night, not since his ex had blacklisted him. As for trying to fix that old banger, he didn't even consider it. He gave the steering wheel a good beating and swore at it with such violence that a prostitute might have blushed. A vertical flashing neon sign turned his red face blue every other second. As he leant through the window, he remembered that he was parked close to the Luník, the hotel at number 50. It was practically opposite number 57. Of course! He didn't have any spare clothes, but he was only going to be there for one night.

Ten minutes later, he moved into a room on the fourth floor, almost face to face with his prey. The hotel was half empty at this time of year, so he'd been able to choose his room. 'The address on my ID card is an old one,' he'd told the receptionist. 'I live in České Budějovice now.' And he'd written a made-up address on the form that he had to fill out. How long did he want to stay? He'd almost said 'Just one night' before changing his mind: 'Can I tell you tomorrow?' 'No problem,' she said. 'You know what it's like in November…'

And now he looked down at Londýnská and his broken-down Skoda. He stood in the shadows, perhaps only fifty or sixty feet from the chess player. In order to avoid being spotted, he hadn't turned on the lights in his room. Then again, he thought, a procession of fleeting neighbours must have passed through these rooms over the years: why would she pay them the slightest attention?

The Luník. Why hadn't he thought of it earlier? He was glad now that the engine had failed. Those Skoda factories in Mladá Boleslav had finally made a positive contribution to human existence.

He'd drawn the net curtains, fearing that the milky light from the streetlamps might creep into his room and betray him. When he looked through his telephoto lens, he felt as if he were in the woman's living room, near the piano. From here, he'd be able to spot any visitors who might be bringing her Chopin pastiches. Not only that, but – with this commanding view of the entrance to number 57 – he could also photograph anyone who went in or came out. It would be good to stay here for a few days. A couple of weeks, if necessary. Novák could afford it.

That evening, Chopinova, as he'd started to call her, must have eaten dinner in her kitchen, on the courtyard side, so that the living room was bathed in soft darkness. At the back, the light from the corridor lit up a yellow rectangle on the floor – the doorway that led to the rest of the apartment. It hadn't taken this former secret agent more than half an hour to go from being a detective to a paparazzo. When he thought that nobody in the world could possibly guess where he was now, he felt a sort of light euphoria that lingered like a woman's perfume. What a thrill it was: not being where everybody thought you were; being where nobody thought you were.

He ate an early dinner at a nearby restaurant and returned to the hotel less than an hour later. He still didn't turn on the lights. In her apartment, everything was the same: just that yellow rectangle at the back of the living room. Beyond the yellow rectangle, he spotted another door. Her bedroom must look out onto the other side, probably onto a courtyard with a few trees or parked cars. She must spend her evenings over on that other side, where it was quieter. In the end, the detective closed the blinds and watched a foreign show on TV Nova while drinking a Budvar. He went to bed early and was soon asleep. In the morning, he regretted not having watched the apartment for a little longer. What if he'd missed the solution to the whole enigma, all for the sake of a few lousy minutes?

XI

WITH THE HELP of the Polaroid and the directions provided by the detective, Ludvík Slaný soon found his way to the gravestone near the arcade gallery, in the north-east corner of Vyšehrad Cemetery. This damp day, with its lingering odour of dead leaves in puddles, had entered the realm of dusk (although it could be argued that November days in Prague were forever in the realm of dusk). The bells of St Peter and St Paul rang for four o'clock. In one hour, the cemetery would close. What was he expecting from this visit? Was he just trying to make sure that the photograph was genuine? Probably. He was a scientific materialist to his core, and he found it almost impossible to believe anything that he couldn't verify with his own eyes. It had not been until his first trip to the other side of the Iron Curtain that Ludvík had admitted that the West was not merely a mirage. Similarly, it was only now, as he touched the nameless gravestone with his fingertips, attempting to detect traces of some ancient letters or dates, as on a runic stone, that he started to believe what the detective had told him.

Mired in confused thoughts, he stood there for a long time before heading regretfully towards the exit, above which he saw the inscription *Pax Vobis*. Peace be with you! If only this case would leave him in peace… He couldn't see a caretaker or a building where one might be hiding. The only nearby structure was home to a café that looked closed. To his right, in a square belonging to a convent, he spotted a nun padlocking a gate after tending to her sisters' graves. Did she know who looked after the cemetery? No, she had no idea. Ludvík walked around the neo-Gothic basilica and found the second entrance without seeing another living soul. He daydreamed about bumping into a gravestone historian, holding an updated register of the dead, so that he could ask the question that was nagging him: who lay under tomb 38 in square 12? Would he be left in suspense to the end? At last, he spotted an elderly man sweeping a paved path, a cigarette stub gripped between his lips. But when Ludvík questioned him, he soon realized – from the man's shrugs and frowns – that he was no archivist. He felt a spark of anger towards the woman who had led him on this wild goose chase. He had fondly imagined that, in this cemetery with its rich history of musical dead, she had perhaps come to kneel at the graveside of some unknown genius who, while still alive, had passed on to her dozens of apocryphal scores, like a shadow of Chopin stretching to the end of the twentieth century. The tomb of the unknown composer… What next? How could he fool himself like this? Was that woman trying to drive him mad?

He walked away from the cemetery along the paved track, between two lines of leafless trees. The city had drawn away from the Vyšehrad hill, like a sea at low tide. No more nuns or visitors come to mourn their dead. Not a sound, other than the whistling of the wind. Even the bells had fallen silent. Was time standing still? The cold made him shiver; it wasn't quite night-time yet, but it was only a matter of minutes. He recalled the legend of the White Lady, in the book that had scared him so much when he was a child, and he began to walk more quickly, holding the collar of his coat tight around his neck. The immense fortress, perched high above the city, was host to so many tales and rumours. How often had he imagined the White Lady hovering in the darkness of the cemetery, and the Headless Horseman, a messenger from Princess Libuše? And now he, too, was adding to the litany of dark fantasies, with this blank gravestone…

The next day, he asked an assistant to do some research on the grave and she laid siege to the telephones of the relevant bureaucratic offices to find out more about the occupant of sepulchre 38, square 12. She called him back that afternoon: the grave had no known owner; nobody was paying for the plot anymore. She'd found out nothing about the name of the person buried underneath that stone. In the end, a suspicious administrator had asked her if she was thinking of buying the plot herself – and, if not, why was she seeking so much information about it?

At this point Ludvík called a pianist renowned for his interpretations of Schumann and Chopin, to whom he had sent some of the scores transcribed by the medium. The man sounded troubled. Yes, he'd had time to examine the pieces. One of them was Chopinesque, but there was something light, even cursory, about it, as it consisted of a repeated series of two chords – tonic/dominant – from beginning to end, with the exception of a few modulations. On the other hand, the mazurkas struck him as much more deeply imagined, and they did resemble certain pieces by the Polish composer. Where had he found them? They were pastiches of remarkable quality. The guy who'd written them must have been a shining light at the Academy of Performing Arts. And the pianist began mentioning the names of a few colleagues whom he vaguely suspected.

The guy who'd written them… If only that old chauvinist had known that a woman was behind the 'pastiches of remarkable quality' that he must have played on his own keyboard… A former dinner lady, in fact… The pianist kept asking and Ludvík remained evasive. He talked about certain discoveries found in an old library in Poland, which the experts had not yet examined in any depth. They'd have to wait a little longer for a definitive verdict… It was possible that the pieces were really by Chopin, but impossible to say for now. Ludvík had been curious about the pianist's opinion because it might be a long time before the experts agreed about the pieces, if they ever did. Ludvík talked at length about doubts that already existed to varying degrees over the authenticity of certain works attributed to Chopin, such as the waltz in A minor KK IV b/11 and the waltz in E flat major KK IV a/14, and even a nocturne (in C minor KK IV b/8), doubts which musicologists had not entirely been able to settle.

Ludvík was unnerved by the pianist's opinion. He had also sent the works to two other 'experts'. If they said that the works were shallow, mediocre pastiches, he could breathe a sigh of relief; he'd put it all down to the supposed medium's subconscious, and

Věra Foltýnova's claims would be torn to pieces. Yet another charlatan would be exposed by the forces of reason and order would return to the world. Oh, how comforting it was to be a sceptic, as soothing as silk sheets…

One of the two musicologists called him two days later. He said he'd immediately recognized Chopin's harmonic path, the hallmark of his work, and that was not to mention the *sfumato* and *rubato* and certain other inimitable tics that only someone with a very deep understanding of the composer's work would know about. He'd also noted Chopin's sense of vision and – these were the musicologist's exact words – the 'organic mastery' of these compositions, which made them something much more than 'mere shallow imitations'. The expert had no reservations in stating that these pieces were very close in style to Chopin and – assuming they were taken from old manuscripts discovered in a likely place – he would not be surprised if they were authenticated as being by the hand of the master himself.

The second musicologist was more mistrustful but reluctant to commit himself. After beating around the bush for some time, he made it clear that his problem was the provenance of the pieces he'd been sent. I'm on the right track, thought Ludvík. This guy's opinion was fundamentally negative, but he didn't want to offend anyone. All the journalist had to do was soothe the man's fears… Having been assured that his words would remain off the record and that the author of the pastiche was not Czech, the musicologist gradually agreed to give his impressions.

'One can sense,' he said, 'that the composer of these pieces admires bel canto, whose "shadow" one can perceive, as in Chopin's *rubato*… He is also an admirer of Mozart, detectable behind a highly Chopinesque rhythmic freedom. As for the *rubato* in the pieces that you sent me, the most expressive notes are especially emphasized... Whoever composed this is very talented. He must have studied counterpoint and different forms in some depth. But, you know, that is a common exercise for students at music schools. There are probably a hundred of us – maybe two hundred – capable of writing this kind of thing. Having said that... there are little elements here that are really specific to Chopin and quite difficult to master. It's surprising. I would be curious to see how these pieces would fare at the Chopin Contest in Warsaw, if it were opened up to pastiches...'

When asked about the instructions written in the margins, the musicologist hesitated, then said this: 'There's something interesting. The bars that are repeated – at the start of the melody – were circled in pencil on the sheets that you sent me. Chopin himself did that, presumably to draw attention to the repetition. You can see it on facsimiles of his manuscripts. Whoever wrote this must be a highly developed mimic.'

'Is it well known?'

'What? The habit of circling repeated bars? To anyone curious enough to look at the facsimiles, yes. There's nothing extraordinary or even very significant about it. It's just a detail.'

So the three experts were more or less unanimous, thought Ludvík, despairingly. Only a slight reservation from the first one, and only about one piece. There was nothing here that he could use as evidence. There was no point pursuing this line of enquiry, other than to drink the chalice down to the dregs, and Ludvík preferred not to do that. If he asked other experts, he would almost certainly get similar reactions. So what did that mean? That they were dealing with a brilliant impostor. It couldn't possibly be Mrs Foltýnova. All three experts said that a rudimentary musical education – as the medium claimed to have received – would make it impossible to compose music of such high quality.

Mrs Foltýnova… That was how he thought of her sometimes now, because despite his despondency, despite his inability to twist reality in the direction he wanted it to go, he was starting to feel a certain respect for her; among all the irritation and bitterness, there was also a degree of admiration.

Just to make his day complete, he also learnt that an internationally renowned British pianist, Peter Katin, had agreed to interpret what Supraphon was cautiously calling 'some pieces inspired by Chopin'. 'Not only is Katin a very experienced musician in his mid-sixties,' Novák said on the telephone, 'but he's a Chopin specialist, which will give their CD a certain credibility. So that's where we are,' he concluded, and Ludvík would have had to be deaf not to hear a hint of reproach in his boss's voice.

This was the coup de grâce. The world of spiritism and charlatanism was now being publicly endorsed by a famous romantic pianist.

'So where are you with your investigation, Ludvík?' Novák asked. 'Any results from the surveillance?' To which the journalist stammered that he needed more time, perhaps more than they'd originally agreed, because, for now, the detective hadn't found out anything. And as for the musicologists…

*

Suddenly there was an earthquake and the ground danced a jig. Everything that Ludvík had patiently categorized inside his mind over the years – everything that, just the day before, he had believed absolutely – was now swaying prettily. From this point on, when he tried to restore some semblance of order to his deepest convictions, nothing would ever be the same. He discovered that there was not one single, unique method to explain the world and to label its infinite number of components. Some of his certainties had started to shake; if they toppled over, they would probably break beyond repair. How long had they been balanced on the edge of the void without him even being aware of it? It was a long time since he'd been in a state like this: a sort of intellectual seasickness, an existential nausea.

The telephone rang.

'Slaný. Who's that?… Ah, Roman. Hello… Yes, that's right, we're meeting the day after tomorrow, ten-thirty at her place… A bit later? I doubt that'll be a problem… Eleven…Okay, I'll check with her and… By the way, about…' – here, Ludvík's voice suddenly fell to a murmur – '… I heard back from several musicologists in the last couple of days… Well, let's just say that they haven't made things any easier… At least there's a certain consistency… No, it'd take too long to explain over the phone… Actually, I'd like to talk with you about it before referring them to Novák, if you… I'm not sure I understand anything anymore… I'd much rather be in your place, behind a camera, filming what I'm told to film without having to ask any questions… You frame reality, you record it, but you don't have to decode or interpret it… Yeah, that'd be great. Thanks for asking… Let's have a drink when you have time, I think I need to talk this whole thing out… About four? Okay, see you then.'

They met at the antiquarian bookshop on Spálená, where Ludvík liked to spend hours browsing. Then they walked down the street and sat in the first café they saw. They were silent while they waited for their Gambrinus. Where to start?

'I went to Vyšehrad,' said Ludvík after the waiter had brought them their beers. 'I saw the nameless gravestone. And then, straight after that, I heard back from several musicologists… They all said the same thing – it was incredible! I was hoping they'd disagree, lay into each other… Or even that they'd unanimously denounce the pieces as forgeries, so we could corner that woman in her lies. But it was the exact opposite. I'm the one who's cornered. I mean, none of them used the word "genius", but they all said it was too interesting to dismiss. They're intrigued and they want to know where I found these scores.'

'So it's not going the way you hoped? They didn't give the verdict you were expecting… Just be patient, because you're sure that our brilliant detective will find proof that it's all a scam sooner or later, right? And then you'll know what cunning genius is pulling the puppet's strings. The puppet that we keep filming in her apartment, day after day…'

'I'm starting to think Sherlock won't find anything, no matter how many stones he turns over. If there was something to find, I feel sure he'd have discovered a clue by now. No, I'm not convinced we're going to turn up anything compromising. Let's wait a bit longer. I was being naive, thinking that this would be fun and easy. If I manage to finish this documentary, it'll just be a good advert for Mrs Foltýnova.'

'Who said "journalism is starting off with one idea and ending up with another"?'

'The documentary isn't really what worries me anymore. Even if I had to abandon it, I'd get over it. That's not the problem.'

'So what is?'

'I don't know. It's like part of me is dying. And I refuse to admit it.'

'You see? You managed to say the taboo word: *dying*. You came into this all optimistic, thinking that you'd bring down the enemy – an artistic impostor – just like people have been doing since the dawn of time, and instead you've come up against a woman who talks about death every time you question her. But not conventional death, not the kind of death that everyone wants to avoid. Not the kind of death that's taboo, that people sweep under the carpet so they don't have to see it anymore. She talks about a kind of death that you find surprising and that, I think, you find hard to hear about. A "happy" death, in a way. And you find that even more disturbing than the death that's hidden like a family secret. Have you never wanted to die… out of simple curiosity?'

'Curiosity? What, you'd kill yourself because you're curious?'

'Out of simple curiosity, yes. Just to find out what's on the other side of that damn closed door, which opens only once for each of us.'

'What do you mean?'

'I mean, to check if there's anything on the other side of the door. And, if there is, to find out what it is.'

'And what if there's nothing? You know, deep down, that there's nothing, right? Nothing but mankind's romantic need to believe we're immortal, to calm our fears and make our existence more bearable.'

'You really think they made that door for no reason?'

'To avoid overpopulating the earth, that's the only reason. It's just a biological rule. And you wanted to commit suicide, just to be open-minded?'

The cameraman gave a slightly forced laugh. In a weak voice, almost as if he were talking to himself, Ludvík went on:

'If I could be sure that my father was waiting for me on the other side of that door of yours… I never knew him, you see… If I could be certain I'd be able to meet him… I'm intransigent when it comes to scientific questions. I'm biologically atheist. But when it comes to him, I'd be ready to believe anything. I'd be ready to risk opening that door.'

'So there you go – dying out of curiosity. What I was trying to explain is that, even if you cling to the idea of a forgery, you can't carry on without talking about death and the mysterious border that separates it from life; and that's the biggest taboo in today's world. Unless you make death miraculous, like passing through a wall. If people are optimistic about it, maybe it stops being a taboo…'

Ludvík was only half listening to Roman, nodding haphazardly. Passing through a wall… He thought about the people who'd emigrated, or been expelled, six or seven years earlier: they caught a train, their passports stamped with the legendary exit visa, promising to write as soon as they reached their destination. They, too, died out of curiosity. Those left behind knew exactly what time in the evening the convoy would stop at the border, in darkness. Soldiers would stand outside every door of every carriage while, inside, guards would examine identity papers and search suitcases, shine torches under seats, wherever they could. Under the carriages too. Especially under the carriages. And then, after a long wait, the train would continue its slow journey towards the other side, crossing the Styx of the modern age. Did the West exist? Back then, he sometimes doubted it. No emigrant ever came back to confirm it. As for the censored letters, the envelopes steamed open and then glued back, there was something hollow, ghostly about them, as if they'd been conceived in one of those back rooms where the regime wrote the fiction that filled the newspapers, and which nobody read except between the lines. Those letters in which nothing could be said, those envelopes with postmarks too beautiful to be true… did they really come from the people who had left?

Ludvík emerged from this deep reverie and paid attention to Roman, who was talking about Virgil.

'… the few men who came back from hell did it centuries ago. In literature,' he explained, 'the Greek and Roman authors weren't afraid of appearing ridiculous, so they never hesitated to send their characters to the land of the dead. Virgil opened the gates of hell to Aeneas and then brought him back; Homer did the same with Ulysses. Then Dante. Nowadays, it's like some intellectual authority has declared that this border is one-way only. You can't come back from hell anymore. Are you listening to me, Ludvík? With her Chopin, Věra Foltýnova is a sort of *aiodos*. That's what you can talk about in your film. It'll be far truer than all those conspiracies that your detective is trying to expose. Foltýnova is our version of Charon, the ferryman who carries souls across the river… She brings them to us, brings news from the other side, and even brings us what they've done on the other bank of the Styx. You need to take the high road!'

'You're remarkably inspired today, Roman. If you're saying this to cheer me up, then thank you.'

'I'm not inspired at all. Have you heard what people say when they come back to life after being almost dead or even brain-dead? We're in such a strange rationalist age, nobody wants to believe what they've seen. In the nineteenth century, when spiritism arrived in Europe, people weren't so cautious. Take Victor Hugo, for example. He and his group in exile: they wrote about their seances, described communicating with Shakespeare, with all the great men of the past… Nobody nit-picks about Hugo because he was a great man himself. He talked to Shakespeare? Okay. To Napoleon too? Sure, no problem. Did he make it all up? Was he sincere? Nobody dares express any doubts. He's Hugo, the great novelist and activist. And he wasn't the only one; he was part of a circle of spirits… One day, Jesus turned up! Not bad, huh? The bigger, the better… But for Foltýnova, the reaction's not the same. Not at all. She's the unknown soldier of spiritism. Not only do we refuse to believe her, but we bring back the StB, the channel pays a spy to follow her around twenty-four hours a day until he detects a false note (no pun intended). You and I face a mass of red tape just to buy a ream of paper, but when it comes to exposing this woman, no expense is spared. Crazy, isn't it?'

*

When he got back home, Ludvík found a surprise waiting for him. 'What are you doing here, Zdeňka?' She'd exhausted the possibilities of sleeping on her friends' sofas while she waited for an apartment of her own. Was she bothering him? 'No,' he told her, wondering if this was actually the complete opposite of the truth. 'It's just that I don't feel very sociable tonight. I'm not really in the mood to talk about our problems or listen to you. Do you know how long you're planning to stay?' She shrugged and raised her eyebrows, a combination that tended to make him fear the worst. 'Yes, the apartment is yours too, until we sell it. The problem is that I live here too, which doesn't make it easy, the way things are…'

She seemed to have come in peace, however. He saw no flashes of anger in her obsidian pupils, no signs of tension on her face. She even dared to smile. Had she called a truce? He would have loved to touch her, to see how her skin reacted. It had been a long time. He needed someone to listen to him. He sighed, and she understood.

'Feeling down, Ludo?'

He cautiously started to speak on a subject that he didn't know much about. Himself. According to Roman, it was Zdeňka's turn to suffer. He'd promised himself he wouldn't mention the subject to her, but he immediately started telling her, for the first time, about the documentary that Novák had commissioned him to make. The slow, stuttering investigation and its disappointing results. His demolished certainties and the discovery of something he found hard to deal with: doubt. The expert opinions, which contradicted all his hopes. The growing hate he felt for Chopin and, deep within his very core, a profound sense of unease.

‘For the first time,’ he said, ‘the thread I’m trying to unravel just keeps getting more and more tangled.’

She seemed interested.

‘He sounds like a tulpa, your composer.’

‘Like a what?’

She gave him some fairly muddled, fragmentary explanations. Although well versed in esoteric orientalism, Zdeňka was not blessed with the gift of clarity, so quite often – as now – she left her ex standing bewildered at the door to her world. He preferred to change the subject. What strange alchemy had the two of them attempted, he wondered: the Zen apprentice and the old-fashioned Marxist? They’d certainly overestimated the power of love! He smiled at this thought; his way of accepting the latest ceasefire.

‘I’ll be leaving in a few days,’ she told him later. ‘I’m looking for an apartment, a flatshare, so don’t worry, I won’t be here long.’

XII

Now it was Ludvík Slaný who stood behind the net curtains in the Luník, a hotel with a name that evoked those Soviet lunar probes. Like the moon, he gazed down at the windows opposite. Pavel Černý, struck down by a nasty bout of flu, had gone back to his suburban apartment. This was convenient for Ludvík, who now had the perfect excuse to leave his own apartment to Zdeňka while she made arrangements to leave for good. He felt like a soldier, all his attention fixed on the enemy trench opposite, his mind cleared of its parasitical thoughts. And, being far from the office, he was spared Roman's homilies, which tended to be more annoying than helpful. He would rather finish this documentary on his own, without the cameraman's intrusive aid.

Sometimes the telephone jingled mournfully. When he was in a good mood or feeling bored, Ludvík would answer it. 'Hello?' This time it was Novák, whom he'd forgotten to keep updated – although it must be said that, in this hotel room, he'd found the ideal spot to practise his procrastination techniques. Although he'd given him carte blanche until recently, Novák now wanted a date. He insisted. For the first time, he began talking about concrete deadlines. Ludvík thought quickly. He asked for another few weeks then invented an excuse to cut short the conversation. 'I just saw her leave the apartment building,' he lied.

With the cold weather, she came out very seldom. One morning, however, he tailed her from a distance, afraid that she would sense his presence. What would he say if she did? The explanations he'd cobbled together were not very convincing, but he had to follow her. Because what if this was the time when it happened? What if, at the end of this walk, he discovered the machination that Černý had missed?

It's easy to become a voyeur. Or rather, you don't become a voyeur; you already are one. Every human being is a spy inside. You'll spy on your neighbour. That morning, after putting on his trench coat, Ludvík followed the elderly housewife as she carried her shopping bag. A grocer's, a baker's. Next, a butcher's? No, because first she swung by a pharmacy and the modest Tylovo Náměstí market. From a distance, he watched the woman's string bag gradually fill with provisions and thought what a pathetic excuse for a secret agent he was. His prey never turned around and pointed at him accusingly, as he feared she would, but he was surprised by a strange thought: watch out, Chopin might see you and snitch on you to the housewife sixty feet ahead! It was like an arrow shot by another mind, an exo-thought that had entered his mind and made him feel ashamed. He shook his head free of it almost as soon as he noticed it in there, but, much later, he was still angry at himself for having paid any attention to the idea, even for a fraction of a second.

When he got back to his hotel room and found the bed freshly made, he had the impression that he'd wasted his time by going for that walk… or, perhaps, worse, that she was giving him the runaround. For the rest of the day, he was assailed by a sense of unease all the more unpleasant because he couldn't work out its origin. A thought returned: there must be something else. But what? The way he was looking at this case was leading him to a series of dead ends. In the most abstract way imaginable – as when you look through a misted window and see silhouettes without faces – he understood that his unease would dog him until he'd figured out a different way of contemplating the situation. In fact, hadn't he already started doing that, somewhere deep inside? Ludvík was like a large ship carried along by its own momentum while, on board, the crew had already begun altering its course. Blinded, he was suffering because he still couldn't see the situation in a new light, but soon that would all change. This idea frightened him. But he knew it was true.

Who profits from this crime? That was the question he'd left unasked for too long, and the one he had to answer now.

In the days that followed, this question absorbed most of his time. Whenever he took a break from his vigil, he devoted himself to his favourite activity: interrogating people, testing theories, thinking… He got it into his head that a music publisher was attempting a major coup with these scores attributed to Chopin; the works of certain composers had recently come into the public domain and the publishers had a desperate need for new sources of money to compensate for this; Ludvík tried to convince himself that this was the crux of the matter. Yet he could find no compelling evidence that Věra Foltýnova was acting as a shield to some venal music publisher. Two young journalists that Novák had put at his disposal in the hope that their aid would hasten the conclusion of the investigation dedicated their days to proving this hypothesis, but it turned out that Mrs Foltýnova had no contract with any publisher whatsoever. As for Černý, some of whose ex-informers now worked in banks, he was categorical: no payments other than her monthly pension had been made to the lady's bank account.

So, who profited from the crime? How had this modest, unassuming woman succeeded in impressing so many journalists and musicologists? What was the mysterious fuel that drove the production of these brilliant scores? What if the whole thing was not motivated by money at all? Yes, perhaps that was it, thought Ludvík Slaný eventually, perplexed and wearied after so many days and nights in this smoke-filled two-star hotel room. Great art, he concluded, crushing his cigarette stub at the bottom of the ashtray: what else can it be? And when, in the afternoon or the evening, he spotted her figure sitting at the piano, playing music he couldn't hear (if only it were summer, and the windows were open...), he felt something quite close to admiration, tinged with brief flashes of rage. Černý had got hold of a copy of the contract between the woman and Supraphon, and it was no smoking gun: the expectations were all quite reasonable, the sums paid to her very modest.

Occasionally he found himself thinking about that conversation with Zdeňka. His ex was a woman of bold intuitions. Yes, he thought, perhaps that was the next angle he needed to investigate. He would dig deeper. He wouldn't tell her anything. Perhaps those words had been her parting gift to him?

Unless Věra Foltýnova had lied to everyone and – as some had suggested – received a considerably more advanced musical education than she claimed. This was all Pavel Černý could cling to as he began tailing her again. And this time he didn't limit himself to the surfaces of streets. Now, she led him deeper into the darkness and he felt like a potholer with a lamp on his helmet, venturing into the chasms of the past. Part of Ludvík's poor brain still wanted to believe that the whole thing was a scam. The journalist had not yet played his last card. That would wait until their next meeting.

XIII

'I DON'T WANT YOU to talk today. Not yet, at least. First, I would like you to listen to a recording. You can listen to it while the camera is rolling, and then react – or not – while it continues to roll. Agreed?' Ludvík asked, without waiting for a response.

For a few moments, there was a look of anxiety on Věra Foltýnova's face that he'd never seen before and he savoured the idea that he had finally managed to unsettle her. Her usual composure deserted her momentarily. Then, as if aware of this weakness, she answered: 'Yes, of course, that's fine…'

As he pressed *play* on the tape recorder, Ludvík felt a surge of confidence: this time, he might actually catch her in his trap. Just then, he noticed the scent of lilac in the apartment, less strong-smelling than usual. He asked the woman: 'Do you understand English?'

'Not very well.'

'That's not important. Forget the words and concentrate on the voice that you're about to hear.'

The tape began to play. The camera began to roll.

After a few seconds, a husky voice could be heard, the voice of an older man who smoked. He was speaking English, trying hard to articulate clearly, with an undisguised Slavic accent that rolled all his Rs. 'Real music, true music, great music is something that exists beyond your world and that comes from the spiritual part of man, from a comprehension of the greatness and uniqueness of God. Great music is something that is only really born in the spirit and reproduced – in a baser form – in your world,' said the voice in a lilting, bantering tone.

Věra Foltýnova didn't bat an eyelid. She listened to the recording as calmly as if it were the weather forecast. Now the voice was talking about the death of the person supposedly speaking. 'All I remember is lying in bed and feeling very ill. Some of my friends were with me and gradually a feeling of peace descended. I felt as if I were drifting away... And then...'

Ludvík pressed *stop*. The camera kept rolling. He said nothing, staring at Věra Foltýnova and waiting for her to speak.

He didn't have to wait long.

'It's the recording made by Flint, isn't it?'

'Exactly. So you've heard it before?'

'No, but I've heard *of* it. I've been expecting someone to play me that recording sooner or later. It's quite old, isn't it?'

'Made in the late Fifties, I believe. And the voice?'

'Chopin? What were you expecting me to say? That I was surprised by it? I've heard that voice almost every day, for years and years. Flint's recording is exceptional because he managed to let other people hear the voices of the dead. Did you think I wouldn't recognize Chopin?'

'When did you first hear about what Leslie Flint was doing?'

'Probably three or four years ago... You know how difficult it was to be sure what was happening, before, on the other side... In the West, I mean.'

'So the voice we just heard is the same voice that you hear, in your apartment, when you're in communication with Chopin?'

'Absolutely.'

'What the hell was that about?' Roman demanded when they were out on the street. 'You pull that voice from beyond the grave out of your hat like some third-rate magician? I know I'm only a cameraman, but if you'd have let me know what you were up to beforehand, at least I wouldn't have looked so shocked. We're supposed to work together, aren't we?'

'Sorry. You're right... Next time, I'll be sure to keep you in the loop beforehand. The idea came to me at the last minute, in fact. Flint was a British pseudo-medium who claimed to be able to summon dead celebrities and record their voices, back in the Forties and Fifties... Oscar Wilde, Churchill, Rudolph Valentino, Gandhi and many others. Including Chopin. Everyone at the channel knows what I'm working on, so someone told me about this guy and I discovered that the radio station archives contain some recordings of these "voices". In the spiritism world, Flint is revered, but in the wider world he has many detractors who point out all the frauds he perpetuated during his career as a con artist. Some say he was a talented ventriloquist. And that he insisted on working in total darkness, which enabled him to have accomplices in the room. Others claim that he used pre-recorded tapes. The guy is generally considered to be a charlatan, and – as you just saw – Mrs Foltýnova said that the voice she just heard is the very same as that of the "Chopin" who visits her.

So there are only two possibilities: either Flint really did record the voices of dead people. In which case, why is he generally considered a fraud? Or… the voice that we heard has nothing to do with Chopin's voice – something that I'm certain of – in which case our friend was shamelessly lying when she told us that she recognized her composer… for the good and simple reason that she never hears anybody.'

'Well, at least she didn't hesitate… She was completely unfazed.'

'True. She doesn't lack composure, I'll give her that. But there's something else about Flint… I didn't play the whole "Chopin" recording, just now. The seances where Flint summoned the voices of the dead were public. At a certain point during the recording, someone in the audience asks "Chopin" to say a few words in Polish, instead of speaking English. The voice answers: "Ah, you want to test me, do you?" The voice laughs, but doesn't speak a single word of Polish. Pretty obvious that it's a fraud, don't you think?'

For the first time, Ludvík had the pleasant feeling of having gained the upper hand. He'd suffered a defeat on the day of the portrait, but now he'd fought back. She had fallen into his trap without even suspecting. It wasn't enough, though; he knew that. It was a strong clue, but it offered no actual proof. He was far from being able to declare to his opponent: 'Checkmate! Now, confess the truth! I want to know who has been giving you those scores…' And if, by chance, she had conceived the whole plot on her own, he would demand to know where and when she became such a brilliant mimic. Had she really told the truth – the whole truth – about her past?

*

Pavel Černý was back at work now, and he had taken over the hotel room from Ludvík. During his convalescence, the detective had carried out a different kind of investigation. He 'went down the mine'. In parallel with the horizontal probe – the journalist tailing the old lady – there had been another, vertical probe. Investigating the woman's past, Černý felt once again the comfort he used to feel when he was employed as a secret police agent. Soon, the blessed time of unlimited voyeurism would be over, replaced by their 'democracy'. Knowing this, he took full advantage of the freedom he still enjoyed to shine as much light as possible into those dark recesses he'd been asked to explore. Just as there are people employed to sweep up litter and dead leaves from the pavements, his job was, and would remain, to sweep away shadows, leaving the enemy of the State nowhere to hide.

Pavel Černý was never idle, and this mission struck him as lighter and more enjoyable than those that had come before, because it wouldn't end in tragedy. His war was over. No matter what he discovered about her past, Věra Foltýnova would not spend the rest of her life in a prison cell. Černý's methods might not have changed, but the consequences had.

Every day, he would report by telephone to Ludvík Slaný, who took notes. Sometimes, the journalist would smile – a smile of satisfaction, or of relief. Other times, he would frown. Things were advancing, it was true, but they were also growing more complicated. They were not advancing in the direction he had hoped, hence the look of disappointment on his face as he held the receiver to his ear. 'Her education? Well, it wasn't much of an education. Věra Foltýnova's results in school were mediocre, and she never entered higher education.' Pavel Černý had been through her school reports: Věra Kowalski had been a remarkably average student, and the chart of her grades was basically just a horizontal line, without even a slight upward trajectory to suggest some vague hope of progress. No, Mrs Foltýnova was clearly not the hidden genius that the journalist was hoping to uncover – he had to resign himself to that. Moreover, the detective could confirm that she really was from a very modest background, and – other than her ability to speak Polish, which was of no use to her at school – she seemed to have had no talents or passions. The detective had tried to find out if she'd ever been enrolled in a music school, in case certain qualities – a perfect ear, a gift for memorization – could have been spotted there. The regime wasn't stingy with funding when it came to discovering a pearl among the rank and file. But his research confirmed that she had not been part of any music classes worthy of the name, either here or in Ostrava. The detective didn't realize that, by saying this, he was plunging the poor journalist into the depths of despair.

Could she have taken private lessons? And, if so, from what age? This was where Černý's research came up against a wall. It was very difficult to state with absolute certainty that she hadn't received any private teaching. Besides, Věra Foltýnova herself had admitted to having a few piano lessons when she was a child. The question was how advanced those classes were. And whether Mrs Foltýnova was lying when she said she'd had a very limited musical education. She had lied at the outset, after all, when she said she had no musical knowledge at all. All the same, Slaný needed to remember that her parents had been poor, and that – according to what Černý had been able to find out – neither her father nor her mother had ever played an instrument.

'How did you manage to find out all that?' When Ludvík asked him this question, Černý smiled with his lips closed. His eyes hid behind a barricade of lashes. He didn't reply.

As for the cameraman, his attitude of accepting the world as it was – and his feigned ingenuousness – really got on the journalist's nerves.

'Anyone can produce pale imitations,' Roman repeated, 'but creating a convincing pastiche is a trick that only experienced musicians can perform, Ludvík. It can be taught; it's a musical genre in itself, and people study it. You could find a whole crowd of musicians in this country capable of composing in the style of Chopin; order a mazurka and they'll deliver it to you, as easily as delivering a pizza. But the reason they can do it is that they've spent years sweating over a keyboard to achieve a certain level of excellence, and that's not the case for Foltýnova, don't you see?'

'Yes, yes, I've already heard all this! So what that means, essentially, is that she doesn't have the musical resources to compose anything Chopinesque with even the slightest bit of harmonic sophistication, right? But what's your point?'

'If you're absolutely wedded to the idea that this is a hoax…'

'What? I'm not absolutely wedded to anything! I'm investigating. And, until or unless I find some proof to the contrary, there is nothing to suggest that the nonsense she serves us when we go to visit her is in any way authentic! All these ghost stories are going to end up driving me insane – and it seems they've already had that effect on you. I never knew you were so naive…'

XIV

CENTRAL EUROPE slowly slid into the heart of winter, as if being pushed down a gentle slope, and low clouds machine-gunned the city with a fine hail that stung people's faces, rattled windscreens in traffic jams, and irritated sanderlings as they flew. Because he wanted to browse in his favourite antiquarian bookshop afterwards, Ludvík arranged to meet Pavel Černý in a café on Spálená. The man who sat across the table from him that afternoon was less the private detective than the former StB agent, and Ludvík realized this from his first words.

'I found something interesting, regarding Foltýnova's husband.'

'Jan? He died about ten years ago, didn't he?'

'Yes, in '84. It turns out that I had dealings with Jan Foltyn for a short while, three years before his death… I was asked to tail him to prove that he was taking part in VONS* meetings. I followed him, several days running, and it didn't take me long to provide my superiors with the evidence they needed. He wasn't a member, just a sympathizer. The VONS was mostly made up

* Committee for the Defence of the Unjustly Prosecuted.

of intellectuals, but it was trying to extend its influence among the working classes.'

'You knew him and you're only telling me this now?'

Černý sat back in his chair and retreated behind a wide smile.

'If you knew all the things that I did during those years but don't talk about, Mr Slaný… As far as Foltyn is concerned, my work was limited to supplying my superiors with the evidence they were seeking, that's all. The dead husband doesn't have any direct connection to this case, so it didn't seem worthwhile telling you that I'd followed him to a nest of dissidents. I may not show it, but I do sometimes feel remorse. My cupboards are full of skeletons. Foltyn went to prison because of me. You knew he'd been behind bars, right?'

'Yes.'

'Back when I was working for the StB, I didn't worry about Jan Foltyn's fate. It wasn't my responsibility. My job, as I told you, was limited to gathering evidence; beyond that, I wasn't curious, partly because curiosity would have got me into trouble, and partly because I just didn't care what happened to the guys who got arrested. But recently, doing my research, I realized that he didn't spend long in detention and that he wasn't even sentenced. No trial, nothing. Three weeks in the slammer, and then he was released. I thought that was surprising. It was abnormal, by the standards of the time. He lost his job, but still, it was a very lenient punishment. Which undoubtedly means…'

'That he cooperated.'

'Exactly.'

'Did he talk about his dissident friends?'

'Normally, each person has the right to look at his own files but not at anyone else's. But I still have some good contacts, and I do them favours sometimes, so I was allowed to look at Foltyn's file. He did agree to supply regular information, but not on his dissident friends, strangely. It has to be said that he was only a bit player in the VONS network. No, the person he agreed to provide information about was… his wife.'

'But she wasn't involved in politics at all, was she? Or am I wrong?'

'No, you're right. She didn't play any sort of active role.'

'What do you mean?'

'Maybe she played a passive role. They knew about her… talents… as a medium. Officially, the regime was atheist; all of its ideas and decisions were based strictly on the principles of scientific materialism. But that was just for show. In reality, things were more nuanced. The story is, when Gustáv Husák felt close to death, four years ago, he confessed to a priest. You see? So, as far as Mrs Foltýnova's talents as a medium were concerned, not only were they aware of them, but they knew that she…'

'Who is *they*?'

'Certain highly placed leaders. People at the top of the ladder, or very close to it. They knew that she was visited by the dead. You have to understand that those people felt constantly under threat. They saw plots everywhere and they were prepared to do anything to thwart them. That was why they asked Jan Foltyn to spy on his wife, to report the names of her visitors and what she heard from the other side. His arrest and the three weeks he spent in custody were probably just intended to make Foltyn cooperate.'

'And it worked?'

'He sent them reports, which I consulted. Those people were probably more suspicious of ghosts than they were of the living. Many of them had blood on their hands. They'd reached the top of the ladder by committing crimes, throwing their "friends" in prison, and forcing them to confess to things they hadn't done...'

'Well, that's all very shocking, but I don't really see how it...'

'They must have feared that their victims would speak to her. Feared their revelations. So many ministers, former comrades, so many opponents, so many committee secretaries, so many tyrants and rising stars were tortured and sent to that other world, or lived the rest of their lives in disgrace after being falsely accused. So, of course, they were afraid that some of the dead would come back to haunt them...'

'But why not just arrest the wife, rather than her husband, if she was the potential danger? Or why not just make her disappear? An accident...'

'They must have thought that perhaps not all the dead were against them. They could have had some supporters there, witnesses. Advisers. Perhaps they were on the lookout for revelations that could help them hatch their own plots. As I told you, they lived in a sort of Shakespearean atmosphere. They, too, must have hoped that a ghost would contact them and spill all its secrets... "Now, Hamlet, hear. 'Tis given out that, sleeping in my orchard, a serpent stung me. So the whole ear of Denmark is by a forgèd process of my death rankly abused..." Can you imagine? Under that regime, Mrs Foltýnova was a communicating door to the past, a revolving door that let draughts of air through carrying lies and truths, conspiracies, resentments, all the weeping pus of human vanity…'

'So you're saying Gustáv Husák and some other high-up phonies took her seriously… In the files on her, was there any mention of "meetings" of that sort?'

'You mean did any of the regime's victims contact her? I found no evidence of that. Would that have been mentioned in the reports, even the secret reports? All the meetings I saw described were with nobodies, probably people she'd known in real life. No member of the elite. No opponents of the regime.'

'Do you think Věra Foltýnova ever looked at her file?'

'She never made an official request. She probably doesn't even know that the file exists. She really had nothing to do with politics.'

'So, in that case, she doesn't know that her husband was spying on her.'

'It's better that way, don't you think? Unless he told her about it when he came out of prison…'

So the brains behind the atheist regime had regarded the Foltýnova enigma with respect. Far from considering her a liar or a lunatic, they'd paid her one of the greatest honours of the era: they spied on her. It didn't have much to do with Chopin, thought Ludvík, and yet… well, perhaps it did, after all. Why had he so carelessly assumed that she was bound to be faking when the communist leaders had taken her seriously?

Ludvík stood up with the preoccupied air of a man looking for his lighter, patting pocket after pocket, and the two men walked towards the antiquarian bookshop. Outside its window, they went their separate ways. Černý watched the journalist disappear inside that Aladdin's cave of old books. What was he searching for there that he couldn't find elsewhere? 'I need to do something here, I'll see you later,' Ludvík had told him, as if to make it clear that he no longer wanted the detective's company. Then he'd vanished behind a shelf. As he walked past the National Theatre, Černý remembered that, a few days before this, Ludvík Slaný had postponed a meeting so that he could visit a library, where he'd spent not only the whole of that day but the following days too.

XV

FOR THE PAST forty-eight hours, Černý had resumed his vigil behind the Luník's net curtains and had seen nothing of any note. Was he doomed to observe the windows across the street and their reflections until the end of time, without ever spotting the suspect's silhouette? The only visitors to the apartment were the two journalists who had commissioned him to carry out this strange surveillance. So much work, so much time spent watching such a boring, predictable existence... Was this his punishment for all the souls he'd sent to prison in the old days? Was he already in hell, or purgatory, damned to eternal imprisonment in a two-star hotel room because, one day in 1981, he provided the authorities with evidence against the man who used to live on the other side of this street?

In the middle of the afternoon, long after the journalists had departed, he saw the light come on in her hallway – a sign, usually, that she was about to leave – and he stubbed out his Sparta in the ashtray. Like a wild animal released from its cage, the detective was outside on the street before she even emerged. She was probably just going shopping in the neighbourhood, but at least it would make a change from the company of his own dark thoughts. He finally had an excuse to leave his little hell and he wasn't about to deny himself that pleasure. He followed as she headed towards Jugoslávská, crossed the road and walked down the pavement on the right. He saw her about to catch a tram so he hurried after her and jumped inside just as the doors were closing. So she wasn't just going shopping in the neighbourhood…

The tram had crossed the river and entered Smíchov when she rang the bell, adjusted her hat in the reflection from the misted window, and stood up. After walking a hundred feet or so, she dived into a doorway and he followed. She walked across a courtyard lined with two-storey apartment blocks. But she didn't go upstairs. On the ground floor, she pressed a doorbell. A little later, Černý read the name on that bell: Daniel Bureš.

Two hours later, Věra Foltýnova reappeared on the street outside and took the tram back the way she had come. He would have had to steal her bag to find out whether there was sheet music inside it… The next day, Černý returned to the courtyard in Smíchov and, as he'd done many times before, performed a simple operation: questioning the neighbours under false pretences ('I'm thinking of renting somewhere in the area, but I'm looking for a quiet place. Do you ever hear musical instruments?'). He knocked at several doors and the inhabitants assured him that, no, there were no musical instruments to disturb the peace around here. So he decided to ring the doorbell in question to ask the same question.

Daniel Bureš was a wary, disagreeable-looking man in his sixties, and Černý was able to get a glimpse inside his home as he gave the man his spiel: he was wondering if this was a quiet sort of place where a professor could prepare his classes and correct papers in perfect tranquillity? But the man was mistrustful and reserved, and the detective, recognizing that kind of fear, forced himself to smile in the hope of coaxing him into talking. In vain.

He wasn't surprised to discover, afterwards, that Daniel Bureš was a former member of VONS. Perhaps a friend of the late Jan Foltyn, he speculated, with whom the widow was now having an affair? Or just friends? What had they been doing in his apartment for two hours while he was pacing the street outside? Given the man's past political affiliations, his file was a goldmine of information. Until joining the committee, Bureš had led a discreet life as a teacher and bachelor. No musical instrument was mentioned, and his modest background wouldn't have enabled him to take private lessons. Once his involvement in VONS had been discovered, he'd been fired from his post and had drifted from job to job, before being accepted back into the teaching profession in the autumn of 1990. Another dead end, sighed the detective, who sent his report to Ludvík with the unambiguous title: *False Alarm*.

Surveillance of the woman's letterbox, which the detective was still performing, revealed nothing suspect. Bills, and a few letters from friends or cousins whose handwriting he learnt to recognize. Just to be sure, he took all the post home with him and steamed open the envelopes with a special machine he had that looked a bit like a pressure cooker. One day, he found an advert for 'the complete works of Frédéric Chopin collected on seventeen CDs at an unbeatable price'.

He kept following her, but the results were so tedious – lots of shopping, a few chess games in Lucerna, a meeting at Supraphon; nothing abnormal – that, in the end, Ludvík told Černý not to bother anymore.

The filmed interviews grew less frequent. It started to feel as if they'd asked everything there was to ask. During one meeting, while the woman went into the kitchen to make them some coffee, Ludvík knelt down under a low table and attached one of those metal grasshoppers – it was the only comparison that came to his mind – with a suction pad and a miniature battery hidden under its abdomen. The microphone was only two centimetres long, with a small antenna, like a tail, and the whole thing couldn't have weighed more than a couple of grams. Viruses, germs, microphones: humanity would always be at the mercy of the microcosmic. One week later, Ludvík discreetly removed the grasshopper and replaced it with a new one. When he got back home, he listened to what it had recorded. It was incredibly boring. The old-fashioned microphone worked perfectly, but all he could hear was Věra Foltýnova talking on the phone or with her daughter, who came to visit her one day. No strange voice emerged from the silence to dictate a waltz or betray a conspiracy.

*

One night during that period, Ludvík had a dream. A storm was creating enormous waves on the river in hell and the ferryman's boat remained docked. Dead souls waited at the port for the storm to abate so they could make the crossing. They sat in cafés and listened to the weather forecast on the radio. In the evening, many of them gathered at the Styx Cabaret, where a man sang bel canto, accompanied at the piano by an elegant, sad-looking young man. The souls whispered to one another that this was Chopin, the composer. What was he doing here? Surely he'd crossed the river long ago? Did he still have dealings with the living? At last, Ludvík found a seat and tried to order a drink, but he couldn't get the waitress's attention. After a while, she finally turned towards him and there was a strident ringing noise in his ears.

As he slowly opened his eyes – passing through that half-state between dreams and waking – Ludvík recognized the waitress. It was Věra Foltýnova. His radio alarm clock flashed 07:50 and Ludvík picked up the telephone, still half asleep. Novák spoke in his bad-news voice:

'Ludvík, report to my office as soon as you get here. There are certain questions that need answering immediately. I want you to give me a full report, so we know where we stand. Čermák will be there. Bring Staněk with you.'

'He's…'

Ludvík didn't have time to finish his sentence because Novák hung up. A simple briefing? He doubted that a progress report would satisfy them. If Čermák was going to Novák's office, it almost certainly spelt trouble. The channel's president appeared very rarely. He couldn't have spoken to Ludvík more than twice since the start of the year.

'Ludvík, things are speeding up and now we're just going to have to keep up with them. We've had confirmation that Peter Katin will record the pieces for Supraphon's CD. They're setting the bar very high... Clearly they believe in this music... And they won't pull any punches when it comes to promotion and distribution. The discs will be on sale in a month and a half. We heard all this from Kučera in the political department; his wife works at Supraphon. So the machine is about to be set in motion... They do things meticulously there. Did Foltýnova tell you that she took a load of tests with Czech psychologists? She also went to Supraphon to meet some professors from the Parapsychology Institute in Utrecht. Apparently she passed all the tests: nothing abnormal, they said. She doesn't have cryptomnesia: she has access to all her memories. According to the Dutch, she's not attention-seeking and has a very stable personality. No mythomania, no propensity for lying. She was examined by some former students of Professor Tenhaeff, who was apparently in charge at Utrecht in the Seventies... So that's what Kučera told me last night. And, of course, they're planning to use all these testimonies to give her credibility. As far as attributing the music to Chopin, they're being very careful: all they're saying is that, given this woman's remarkably balanced personality, this is one of the most interesting cases of musical mediumship they've ever come across. So, there you go. That should spice things up...' Novák gave a deep sigh. 'We've given you as long as we can, Ludvík. Now it's time for you to deliver the goods. We need to know where things stand. What angle will this documentary take?'

'Well... To be honest, I still don't have enough information to really take a stance on either side. What we've got is very interesting – fascinating, really – but I still haven't found the evidence that the whole thing's a fraud, and...'

'After all this time, you still don't have a clear idea? What have you been doing? All the means at your disposal and you're still asking for more time?'

At that precise moment, it occurred to Ludvík that the trap was probably closing on him. So perhaps it hadn't just been his paranoia, before... Novák had lured him into this position weeks before, out of bitterness – maybe even hatred – over Zdeňka. It seemed certain now: Novák knew about them. And Ludvík had carelessly stepped onto a flimsy trapdoor made of branches and leaves that was collapsing under his weight; his tormentor, eyes sparkling, was watching him fall and, just to make sure that his humiliation was complete, had invited Čermák to witness it too. All the same, Ludvík didn't panic. Perhaps the glimmer he had glimpsed a few days before was the light at the end of the tunnel? Not only did he not panic, but he felt confident that perhaps, in the end, the trap wouldn't close its jaws around him – at least, not in the way that Novák hoped.

'Give me a little more time. After that, I'll be in a position to give you a definitive answer. To tell you whether she's lying or not.'

Surprised, the cameraman turned to Ludvík, but said nothing.

'And you'll also be able to tell us if the whole thing is a hoax?' Novák asked doubtfully, suspiciously.

'Yes.'

'How much more time do you need?'

'Let's say two weeks. The filming is complete. Well, almost.'

'But you know that Roman will be busy with other stuff from tomorrow. He has deadlines to meet. How will you manage?'

'I'll get by on my own, for a few extra interviews.'

'Okay, I'll give you two weeks – and not a day more. And two weeks from today, you will debrief us, we'll talk it through, and we'll settle on a date for the show to be broadcast. How long will it take to edit? Any idea? You'll have to do it quickly. There's no point turning up at the battlefield after the other side's already won. That happens too often around here. I'll be the one who gets the blame if this documentary isn't ready in time.' Novák turned towards his boss as he said this and smiled, as if to signal that the meeting was over.

After that, Roman and Ludvík went down to the lobby. They each lit a cigarette. Small, hard snowflakes were pattering nervously against the bay window. Looks like winter is here, thought thousands of people all over the city at that moment, as they pulled back their bedroom curtains.

'So what the hell is going on?' the cameraman asked. 'Can you tell me now? I don't hear from you for days, you lock yourself away in libraries, you interview God-knows-who, you keep postponing the editing, all without telling me if you still need me or if I can move on to my next job. What's wrong with you at the moment? Tell me what's going on!'

'You'll find out soon, Roman. I think I may have an explanation. Or maybe *have* is the wrong word. I feel like I'm starting to *glimpse* an explanation. But don't worry. You've done your part. The mist that surrounds me is shifting all the time. Sometimes it thickens and sometimes it drifts away. It won't be too long, though, before it's completely lifted.'

Their last collaborative act was to interview, separately, Věra's two children. Jaromil Foltyn, whom they met at a café in the centre of town, refused to appear on camera and wasn't very forthcoming.

'Did your mother ever have an accident that might have caused a partial memory loss?'

'Not that I know of.'

'Have you inherited her abilities?'

'No… Well, I did as a very young child. Then they faded, until there was nothing left. I don't regret that. I just wanted to lead a normal life.'

Jana, the sister, agreed to be filmed. She thought carefully about each question, taking the time to weigh her words, then answering quite frankly. To the questions that had already been put to her brother, her answers were more or less identical. Several phrases, however, stood out, and Ludvík noted them down.

'My mother is the humblest person I've ever known. Where she grew up, nobody did anything to attract attention. The last word I would choose to describe her is *ambitious*. She accepts everything that happens to her very naturally, as if she were expecting it. She's the total opposite of a compulsive liar… She's a very calm, stable woman. I've never seen her get angry.'

Her lunch break was almost over. Jana Foltýnova had to return to the shoe shop where she'd worked as a saleswoman since leaving school. The two journalists thanked her and walked to Roman's car to put their equipment in the boot.

'They both believe she's completely sincere.'

'You don't think they're protecting her, helping her to pull the wool over our eyes?'

'No. Do you?'

'No,' Ludvík said, without hesitation. There was a silence, then he said: 'I think the die is cast.'

*

Ludvík Slaný spent the next few days working feverishly, making only brief appearances at the office. He announced that he was going to Dresden to interview some German experts. Experts in what? He didn't say. The solution he'd glimpsed fascinated him; it took up all his time and energy. Without realizing, he was becoming exhausted. He went through some strange moods then, which he recovered from after consulting a doctor and getting some rest. He felt like he was on borrowed time. Finally, what he feared came to pass. Novák called him, sounding impatient. He was sick of excuses. He demanded to know. What was happening with the editing? Ludvík didn't feel brave enough to tell him that he hadn't reached that stage yet.

'Well, *they* haven't been wasting *their* time! They've just brought forward the CD's release date. There are concerts planned for next month and they've started promoting them… So I need a broadcast date! Now. We can't wait any longer, Ludvík. Where have you been, anyway? You were supposed to come to the editorial meeting to brief us on your angle, your conclusions.'

Ludvík Slaný took the plunge. 'I'll be there on Wednesday morning, okay? For the nine-thirty meeting. I promise. And we'll finalize everything then – the dates and so on. It took me longer than I expected, but I understand it all now. I'll explain everything when I see you. I'll tell you whether or not Věra

Foltýnova saw Chopin and who wrote the pieces that will be played at those concerts.'

'All right, Wednesday morning it is. But no more delays, you understand? You've kept us waiting long enough.'

'I'll be there, Filip. Without fail.'

PART THREE

XVI

He'd been intrigued ever since he'd first heard her silky-smooth, fast-flowing voice on the telephone. Listening to her, he'd imagined a tall young woman with dark hair, possibly blue eyes, early thirties, maybe… certainly not older. Pretty? He had a feeling she was, but he would have to find that out later. She was talking about making a new documentary for a rival channel to mark the tenth anniversary of Věra Foltýnova's death. And she wanted to see him, not to interview him but to hear his testimony, as a judge might put it, to have a chat as colleagues. To 'follow in your footsteps' as she explained somewhat ceremoniously. He'd thought she was very charitable towards his own investigation. But it was all so long ago… Why stir things up now, so close to the end of his career? He'd hesitated.

The café where they agreed to meet overlooked the riverbank. The Foltýnova affair was twenty years ago and a lot of water had flowed under the bridge, whose dark sentinels he observed now, standing as ever on their pedestals. Would the stranger with the silky voice be punctual or fashionably late? Wouldn't it be better, in the long run, if she didn't turn up at all? 1995–2015: so much water had gone under the bridges of his hometown between those two dates... Several years as a correspondent in Berlin, a few more in Vienna. A marriage, a divorce. And now, he had recently taken over Filip Novák's former position at the channel. At the end of the day, the documentary that Novák had commissioned him to make had not harmed him. Perhaps it had even brought a touch of whimsy and originality to a career that had, by his own admission, been otherwise quite dull.

Ludvík had deliberately arrived early so that he would be free to choose a table with a view of the river. The water level was high, the river almost overflowing its banks, and its surface was littered with floating branches torn from flooded ground upstream. The river flowed quickly, never quite managing to sweep away the city's reflection. Was he waiting for the city to drift downriver? For its reflection to descend to the sea? He would have liked to write a story about that if only he were a better writer; a story in which the reflection of every city in the world was carried away by its river, drifting down to the next city.

Every time a single woman appeared in the café, he started and thought: is it her? He liked these moments: little airlocks of uncertainty before a meeting of this kind. He liked feeling his senses alert, these pockets of time when anything seemed possible. Seeing her enter, he knew from her voice that it was her, and that she wouldn't be indifferent to him, and he promised himself that he would drink as little as possible that evening, so that he wouldn't lose sight of their age difference. For once, his imagination had not led him astray, unless she'd dyed her hair dark brown and was wearing blue lenses in her eyes just to satisfy him. Dana Růžičková, he murmured, standing up to wave to her. Less than five minutes later, he ordered his first beer, and so did she. They began with small talk. He liked her voice and he wanted to hear her talk, to find out who he was dealing with. She was tall and slender but still shapely, and with a charm that made him think irresistibly of Hitchcock's maxim that he didn't like women who wore their sex appeal around their neck like baubles. Dana certainly didn't do that; her sexuality was not on display in that part of her anatomy. He liked her voice, yes, but he was also impressed by the agility of her mind, her ability to analyse situations immediately, perhaps in part because he himself was so different; Ludvík was more like an underground river, taking time to think before resurfacing in a conversation. He enjoyed her quick, humorous repartee, but at the same time he feared one day becoming the target of her wit, as if Hurricane Dana were a storm of intelligence that would one day wreak havoc on his coastline. So the conversation meandered around various subjects, and it was not until half an hour later that Věra Foltýnova was mentioned for the first time.

'In 1995, Dana, back when Novák commissioned me to make that documentary, there was no such thing as email or the World Wide Web, and that made my task a lot simpler. After the first interviews with Věra Foltýnova, I came to the conclusion that this woman had created a perfect system and that only some good old-fashioned espionage would enable us to see through it. I wanted to know who she was mixing with. Among the living, I mean. Novák was of the same opinion as me: a woman from such a modest background who played the piano like a removal man couldn't possibly be operating without some hidden accomplice. Chopin's music is so complex, it was unthinkable that she could imitate it at all, never mind produce hundreds of pieces. No, this Foltýnova woman had to be the figurehead of a masterful artistic swindle, and I fully intended to expose it. From then on, my investigation became a sort of treasure hunt…'

Ludvík Slaný went on this way for a while, carried along by his own momentum, before thinking that the woman probably knew all this already, that she'd read it, probably more than once, and he must be boring her with all these preliminaries. He changed tack.

'But now let me tell you a few things that you don't know about my documentary, Dana. Let me reveal to you its hidden side. Perhaps you saw the news last year about Mamoru Samuragochi? The name doesn't ring a bell? Well, listen, because personally I found this fascinating. He's a contemporary composer known as the "Japanese Beethoven" because he became completely deaf. He was also called the "digital-age Beethoven" because he wrote music for video games. Samuragochi became famous in his homeland with his No. 1 Symphony *Hiroshima*, named after the city where he was born in 1963 to parents who had survived the atomic bomb. He took his first piano lessons at four. A few years later, he could play Mozart and Beethoven. As an adult, he began composing classical music, film music, and – as I've already mentioned – music for video games. By the age of fifty, he had lost his hearing completely. He described his deafness as a gift from God because it allowed him to be more attentive to his own depths. The CD of his *Hiroshima* symphony sold two hundred thousand copies and was even played at a concert for the

G8 leaders a few years ago. Then another of his compositions, a sonatina for violin, was chosen as the music for a Japanese figure skater at the Winter Olympics in Sochi… So, fortune was smiling on this man, and he looked the part too: long hair, dark sunglasses, serious face, black suits. And his deafness was the cherry on top! It was perfect. He was the icon of an era.

'Except that… last year, just before the Sochi Games, the house of cards collapsed. The house collapsed because the cards were rigged; Samuragochi's dark sunglasses hid the eyes of a charlatan. The prolific composer admitted that he'd never composed anything, except at the very beginning of his career, and he apologized for the fraud during a press conference. For almost twenty years, nobody had suspected a thing.

'He confessed,' Ludvík Slaný went on, watching his interlocutor closely to judge the effect of his story, 'because the man who had been secretly writing all the compositions, a music teacher by the name of Takashi Niigaki, was getting cold feet about the arrangement and had threatened to go public with the truth himself. This "ghostwriter" had been working for the impostor since 1996. First, he'd just given him a hand, as his assistant, and then, gradually, he'd taken on all the actual work of composing, in return for money… But a moment always arrives, with this sort of case, when the ghostwriter rebels and throws away his mask. Niigaki couldn't stand the idea that his music would be played at the Olympics and that the whole world would think the skater was dancing to notes composed by someone else.

'Soon after Samuragochi's confession, his ghostwriter confirmed the whole story. He went even further, revealing that the impostor had feigned his deafness, that he could hear as well as you or me…

'When I read the articles about this case last year, I thought of Věra Foltýnova. Back then, in 1995, I was firmly convinced that, sooner or later, her ghostwriter would emerge from the shadows and claim paternity of these works attributed to Chopin. Why? The lure of profit – because the CD would soon be released and the concerts would take place – or simply because he wanted the spotlight to himself. How many people could resist that sort of temptation? But, not only could I not wait forever for this revelation, I wanted to be the one to break the news. I wanted the scoop. But my deadline was growing closer and closer, and my superiors were putting me under constant pressure. It was making me ill. I couldn't sleep anymore.

'So, at this point – the documentary was almost complete and it had to be edited – part of me believed the theory of this brilliant ghostwriter hiding in the shadows, waiting for the perfect time to emerge into the light. The problem was that, while that perfect time might have been a matter of days away, it might also have been weeks or even months. And what if he never showed himself? Would that mean that he didn't exist? Or would it mean that the ghostwriter was dead, which would of course make him the perfect ghostwriter because he would never be able to reveal himself? I was still intrigued by that gravestone without a name at Vyšehrad Cemetery. What lay beneath it? *Who* lay beneath it? If the ghostwriter was already dead, there had to be clues somewhere… letters… something, I didn't know what, but I had to get my hands on them. At the same time, another part of me was starting to follow a new path, which was leading me to see things in a very different light.

'So I was split in two, you see. Depending on my mood, depending on how my research was going, one side would dominate and then the other would get the upper hand. It was a fight to the death. One *me* had to destroy the other *me* before I could escape the exhaustion and illness caused by my indecision. I was running out of time to let the situation resolve itself in my mind, so I had to force things. That was why I decided to call Černý, the detective, one last time.

'Fate was on our side. Věra had to go to London for a few days for a round of interviews and small concerts organized by the record company. In the meantime, Černý was once again staying in his fourth-floor room at the Luník. One evening, we were watching in silence from behind the net curtains. The windows of Věra's apartment were dark, and so were her neighbours' windows. The people in that building were mostly elderly, and apparently they were all asleep. Just after midnight, we decided the time was right. Věra's children would never come to water the plants at that time of night! Pavel couldn't afford to make a mistake; the regime he served before was no longer there to protect him. But he seemed confident. I have to admit, though, that if we'd really thought about what we were risking, we would never have done it. I hadn't told anyone at the channel what I was up to, and if I'd been caught, Novák wouldn't have lifted a finger to help me.

'We had the whole night ahead of us, and we knew from experience that the floorboards in her apartment didn't creak. There were overshoes for visitors just inside the door, so we would slip them on over our stockinged feet. All of this was borderline ridiculous, of course, but without this raid, I didn't think I'd ever be able to decide between the two *mes*. The fate of all those weeks of filming, tailing, phone-tapping and other forms of surveillance would all depend on what we saw at the end of a torch beam. If a ghostwriter was communicating with her, I was bound to find some trace of their communication in her apartment.

'As I said, though, I had imagined a third possibility: that the ghostwriter was dead and buried. If that was the case, he couldn't have departed this world without leaving some clues. Consciously or subconsciously, a ghostwriter always leaves his "signature" somewhere, so that one day his existence might be discovered. It's a rule of survival. Even B. Traven, that mysterious writer who seemed to erase every trace of himself as he moved through life, did actually scatter a few clues, as if a small part of him wanted to cast away the mask. We also had to be on the lookout for the mistakes that all humans make, the little mistakes that go on to betray them and make all attempts at hiding futile.

'So, about twelve-thirty, we went across the road. We didn't have a key, of course, but that didn't pose a problem to Černý. None of the other apartments had a view of the one we were breaking into, so no nosy neighbours could watch us through their spyholes. In less than ten minutes, we were inside. We had the whole night ahead of us.

'We had to act like ninjas, moving silently so we didn't make the downstairs neighbours suspicious. And we had to put everything back exactly the way it was, so the medium would never know we'd been there. The adrenaline rush this gave me was pretty satisfying: I'd long dreamt of crossing the border between journalism and espionage, a border that some of my colleagues would occasionally cross while investigating more dangerous stories.

'It was around one in the morning when we began the inspection in earnest. Gangsters who crack open a safe and stuff wads of cash into their pockets must feel something similar to what we felt then. Although we weren't quite at that stage yet. We'd opened the first door, but there were other doors behind it. Deep down, though, I wasn't worried. I felt like that night would decide everything: depending on what I found (or didn't find), I would choose one of the two *me*s. Never in my life had I been so dependent on a clue.

'Nothing could escape our vigilance: none of the drawers were locked, as if the apartment's occupant had nothing to hide. Or as if that was the impression she wanted to give.

'After checking all this, we set to work. Pavel Černý inspected the flat for a hiding place that I might not have spotted, and after that I assigned him the bedroom and the kitchen. I took what used to be the husband's office when he was alive; the children's former bedroom, now converted into a guest room and utility room; and the living room – where the piano was.

'Věra Foltýnova's handwriting was very distinctive, which made my task easier as I searched by torchlight. It was clumsy and slanted – the calligraphy of someone who'd never done much writing after leaving school. The letters were elongated, reminiscent of calligraphy from the Middle Ages, when most writing was done by monks. They were copyists, and so was

Věra, in her way: a copyist for a ghost. The instructions on the sheet music were handwritten. The notes had something of the letters' long, pointed style; the orbs imperfect, more like rhombuses or pentagons than spheres. From time to time, I would pause and look across the street to the dark room that served as our watchtower. As I went through the woman's post, in search of a single score that wasn't in her hand, my perplexity grew. If we didn't find anything by the end of the night, I would have no choice but to abandon the idea that Věra Foltýnova was a scribe and a screen for some hidden composer.

'We worked for hours like that, slowly and meticulously. I didn't skip a single line. The oldest letters went back fifteen or twenty years. Two of them had been written by her husband, during his time in prison. Occasionally, a car would drive through Londýnská, reminding us that civilization had not completely disappeared. The engine sounds were muffled even as they grew closer, and then they faded to silence as the vehicles moved down Jugoslávská. Nothing I read had any relevance to Věra's supposed gifts. Nothing concerning music, anyway... Perhaps all these people who had, at one time in their lives, felt the desire or need to write to her, were now dead.

'I also went through the receipts for the apartment and the husband's payslips, just in case some important document was hidden between them. From upstairs, I could hear someone snoring, loudly and regularly for the most part, but suddenly falling silent now and then, as if the sleeper's heart had stopped beating for a moment.

'And then, in this slow-motion world, at four o'clock precisely, something happened. The telephone rang. Back then, of course, there was no such thing as caller ID. Who could it be, at this hour of the night? Who needed so desperately to reach Věra Foltýnova but was unaware that she was abroad? Instinctively, Pavel and I looked at each other, and I have to admit that there was fear in our eyes. Answering the phone would have been an act of insanity, and yet it was so tempting. We didn't say a word, but we both had the same thought: what if it's him? The man we were tracking, the improbable, the evanescent, the dark matter of this case. We shook our heads… It was probably just a wrong number. I turned to the window, though, and observed the windows of the Luník, as if she weren't in London at that moment, but over there, in the room that we'd just vacated.

'The telephone fell silent. It had only rung four times but, in the dense and silent time of that night, each ring had chilled us and had seemed to go on for much longer than it really had. Our senses alert now, we went back to our search. I had the impression that I was being watched, and I wanted to get out of there. Did that impression come from the faces on the walls, staring at us with their inscrutable smiles? Or did it come from something else?

'Naive as I was, I kept hoping right until the end that I would find something there. A private logbook, for example, detailing all the journalists like me who'd fallen into her traps, or perhaps listing all her visitors from beyond the grave.

'We slipped away before dawn. After that, I remember sleeping all day. The next morning, we found out the truth about that nocturnal phone call. It had come from abroad. From the hotel in London where Mrs Foltýnova was staying.'

*

'She came back from London two days after our break-in. We'd found absolutely nothing. Although it was now obvious that my hopes were in tatters, I still didn't want to surrender. I wanted to keep fighting. *Just one last time*, as people always say when they can't manage to give something up. Alone now, I continued my vigil from the room in the Luník. I never thought to ask the receptionist whether the hotel was named after the first lunar probe, launched one day in 1959. For my part, I felt as if I were observing the star Foltýnova, as if I had entered her fiendish gravitational field and was desperately trying to glimpse the dark side of that celestial body. Circe held me back, but I gave myself a strict deadline: only two more days of surveillance, and then I would accept the obvious.

'I was anxious. I knew time was running out. The day after her return, she left her apartment in the middle of the afternoon and I wondered if she was going to see that guy – her husband's old friend. She wasn't carrying a shopping bag. I let her get a good hundred feet ahead of me. She was strolling along, window shopping, and she seemed to have time to kill. There was a hint of spring in the air that day; my morning surveillance had been punctuated by two large V formations of migrating birds, those Vs that spread out or contract like banners with the changing seasons. I felt like the sky was mocking me, tracing the first letter of the name of the woman I was following.

'She didn't go to see that guy. The route she took had not, to my knowledge, figured in any of the detective's reports. It was a strange trip, made up of right angles and loops, as if she were navigating by guesswork. She made me think of a character in an American novel whose walk around New York spells out a message on a map.

'After a while, though, she started walking straight ahead, paying no attention to the shop windows she passed. Evening fell. The streetlamps glowed like pearls in the night. Offices closed, the pavements filled with people going home, and I feared I was going to lose Mrs Foltýnova in the crush. I saw her crossing the Palacký Bridge then continuing along Lidická, before turning onto Nádražní and walking more quickly. She obviously knew where she was going. At number 108, she came to a stop outside a little restaurant on the corner of Jindřicha Plachty. After briefly consulting the menu, she went inside. It's very early for dinner, I thought, observing the restaurant's unprepossessing facade from a distance. Why had she gone there? To start with, my gaze was fixed on the front door. Then I glanced at the restaurant's sign and I was dumbstruck. It said: RESTAURACE U LUDVÍKA.

'I recoiled, then crossed the street and took refuge in a bar. I watched the restaurant's entrance from there. Perhaps it was just a coincidence, after all? The human mind has a gift for self-deception. All the same… Walking all the way across the city to eat an early dinner at a third-rate restaurant… Half an hour passed. Forty minutes. Less than an hour later, she came out alone. I'd been hoping to see her in the company of a stranger. Unsurprisingly, she left Smíchov, crossed the river, and walked back home. She'd played a trick on me. She wanted me to understand that, no matter how hard and how long I searched, I would never find anything. It was her way of telling me that she had nothing to hide. But how the hell had she known that I was following her?'

XVII

'It was a nightmare, giving up on the idea of unmasking an impostor, but it was a liberation too. The other path I'd started following didn't seem solid or developed enough to me, and in that unpleasant state of hesitation, some unusually dark thoughts swooped down and engulfed me, like a sudden downpour. I'd booked the editing suite and, to buy myself some time, I'd informed Novák of the dates, but I could feel his impatience. Why was I asking for more time yet again when I'd already told him that the filming was done? I promised to attend an editorial meeting the following week to give a detailed account of the documentary in front of the department heads and the channel's senior management. Yes, I would tell them unambiguously whether or not Věra Foltýnova was lying. But, for now, I preferred not to say.

'I don't know who was spreading the rumour that I didn't have any answers, but whoever it was seemed to have insider access to my state of mind. I knew it wasn't Roman, because he was now busy filming something else. I also knew he probably felt that what he'd accomplished with me had been stolen from him, so I avoided all contact with him. Journalists are often individualists, but where this particular job was concerned I felt even more alone than usual, in terms of my thoughts and decisions. And in terms of my doubts, obviously. For my last interviews – with a psychiatrist, a neurologist and a biologist – I used a trainee cameraman, because trainees don't ask questions. Roman wouldn't be there to sulk or argue. I realized that I was being "unfaithful" to him in some way. He was a very straightforward guy and he held a grudge against anyone who didn't play by his rules. Our relationship was bound to suffer as a result, but I was willing to pay that price in order to pursue my objective. I didn't want anyone putting a spanner in the works, and I knew Roman well: when he didn't agree with you, he would argue his case and he wouldn't compromise, even if it meant abandoning the whole project. I didn't want the documentary to end in a blaze of explanations and insults.

'Those interviews allowed me to glimpse a light at the end of my own tunnel, but I still wasn't sure that it was more than a mirage. Not yet. The tunnel I had to squeeze through was desperately narrow and there was no guarantee I would make it. If only my poor mind had something certain, concrete, definitive it could cling to... but the path I was advancing along was crumbling, unstable. What I saw, I could not yet put into words, into an argument that would be understood by others, and at times I felt I was still a long way from being able to do so. And if I advanced too far through this crumbling landscape, there was a chance I might lose my footing...

'That's exactly what must have happened to me, at home one night. Didn't I sense it coming? Did I really not notice the pressure I was putting myself under, with no way of sharing the burden? Perhaps it would have helped if I'd spoken to Roman, but he was at the other end of the country, absorbed by a project which he must have found much more satisfying than our weeks tracking the medium together. Besides, how would he have taken it? As for Zdeňka, she was no longer coming to my apartment. A few of her clothes still hung in the wardrobe, and a few of her books still lay open on the shelves, as if to spread the scent of nostalgia throughout my home. But I was elsewhere, unaffected by them.

'It happened one night when I was brushing my teeth, eyes closed. I always close my eyes when I brush my teeth, but I shouldn't have done it that night. I didn't see it coming. What, exactly? I don't know. The sensation of a hand on my shoulder. I threw a punch into thin air and snapped my eyes open. Nothing. The bathroom door was closed. It had lasted only a fraction of a second, but it was enough to put me in a cold sweat. I decided it was time for all this to end. As soon as I got into bed, I burst into tears. I felt completely numb, as if my body could move only to perform its most basic functions – eating, drinking, breathing, and that was all. I didn't turn out the light that night. I put it down to stress, and I did eventually fall asleep around dawn. When I woke, everything seemed back to normal. The sun shone softly through the windows. What had happened to me? Was it Zdeňka ghosting into the apartment, playing tricks on my mind?

'None of this made any sense. Besides, I was sure she wasn't coming here anymore. That she would never come here again. I felt hollow and I didn't realize it. Hollow, empty, with no other goal in life than to hide from myself for a little longer the reality of the state I was in.

'The next night began with a long, formless period of insomnia, as if my mission was to stay awake and watch something from my bed. I felt anxious, and the time I spent waiting to fall asleep seemed nebulous, endless. My head was spinning with the interviews I'd done that day, and I crushed those piles of words like grapes to see what came out. The bells of the neighbourhood church tolled two o'clock, then three o'clock, and I lay motionless in my bed, a horizontal sentinel. I heard the bells toll four times and then my mind entered a tunnel of strange dreams. I was asleep at last, tossed from dream to dream. Suddenly I heard myself screaming. I hyperventilated with terror. At the end of my bed, something was firmly gripping my right foot. A hand grabbed my ankle… Where was I? Still in a dream or back in reality? If this was a nightmare, it was so realistic that I believed in its reality. And when I opened my eyes, I felt the hand still gripping me. I turned on the bedside lamp and the grip suddenly loosened. Had I finally woken up, after several seconds of confusion? I sat up, listening closely, staring at the far end of the bed. I couldn't hear anything, except the pounding of my heart. I bent down to look under the bed, just like I used to do every night when I was six or seven. I felt reassured, but at the same time I said to myself, for the first time: Ludvík, you have to do something, quickly. It can't wait… Had I been fully awake when I felt that iron fist? Or had I fallen victim to a particularly realistic dream that had borrowed the backdrop of my bedroom to fool me into believing it? I was still so shocked that I couldn't answer that question.

'No job, no documentary, nothing in my life had ever plunged me into a state like this before. No single word could describe it. It was like a combination of terror, dispossession and powerlessness, but even those words couldn't quite articulate how I felt, sitting there idiotically in the middle of my bed, assailed by I-didn't-know-what. Even the scandal surrounding the article I'd written about Sholokhov hadn't shaken me this badly. I called to book an appointment with a doctor later that afternoon. When I told him about feeling the hand on my shoulder, then being woken by a hand (the same one?) around my ankle, he nodded, then raised his glasses and, without waiting for me to finish, said in a gentle voice: "You're very tired, Mr Slaný. You probably aren't aware of how much stress you're under. But don't worry, all you need is something to calm you down." I saw him write down the Aztec or Sub-Carpathian name of a medicine intended to free me from this state. He believed the sensations I'd felt were purely due to my fatigue and confusion. "You were shocked by those sensations, and that's understandable, but there's nothing surprising about them, considering the state you're in. You must get some rest."

'I'd never taken tranquillizers before and they left me feeling dazed, cut off from part of my memory. Even words, when I needed them, seemed very distant. I had to slowly search for each one. When I told Novák about my condition, for example. He quickly understood what was going on from my voice and my long hesitations. "One week?" he repeated, after calculating something. I could tell he wanted to unleash his fury on me, but he was holding back. There wouldn't have been much point. I was too numb and vacant to feel anything anyway.'

XVIII

'AFTER A FEW DAYS, I started to feel better. Stronger, more sure of myself. The pills I was taking sorted the wheat from the chaff in my neurones; I could see clearly again. Locked in my apartment, I had time to work out roughly what I would tell them. I felt ready.

'It was a perfectly ordinary editorial meeting, with one difference: everyone stayed until the end, so they could watch me. I'd noticed people staring at me questioningly as soon as I arrived in the office. They didn't dare ask me anything directly, perhaps out of fear that they'd be disappointed prematurely. I knew them all well. Some of them were hoping I would take a certain stance on the Foltýnova enigma. Because of the likely viewing figures, or because their intellectual predilections inclined them that way. I knew which ones wanted to hear that Věra Foltýnova really was visited by the ghost of Frédéric Chopin, and which were expecting me to defend and illustrate the theory that she kept repeating with her unfading composure. There weren't many of them. Journalists tend not to be whimsical in that way. Others, still for reasons to do with the viewers or their own entrenched rationalism, hoped for a whiff of scandal, for the unmasking of a gigantic hoax; I counted Novák among their number. I hadn't told anyone about the nature of my conclusions, not because I wanted to prolong the suspense or get as much attention as I could, but because, for as long as I had been turning over that question – in other words, until two days before the meeting – my mind had been so agitated and muddled that clear thinking had been impossible. My brain was a soup of particles in suspension, sometimes shaken by unpredictable eddies that only muddied the waters even further. I hadn't slept a wink all night, going through my arguments like a general the night before a battle – because what awaited me *was* a kind of battle. Victory would mean imposing my views, convincing all the others.

'I was dealing with old hands, journalists whose credo was to get the information and cross-check everything. They didn't simply believe whatever they saw. St Thomas should be the patron saint of journalists. To be honest, I was intimidated by them. I didn't want my exposé to crash on the rocks of their scepticism. I considered several different ways of presenting what I had to say, but in the end I did it off the top of my head.

'"I've finished investigating and filming the documentary I've been working on for quite some time now, and I'm about to start editing it. I imagine you all know broadly what it's about. I'm sure you've all heard about this woman who claims to be a medium who is visited by Chopin so that she can take dictation of his posthumous works. She is going to become more and more famous in the coming weeks, not only here but in other countries too, because she's become a phenomenon: the general public is fascinated, and the experts can't agree. I've come here today to answer the question that I think many of you are asking: does Věra Foltýnova really receive visits from a composer who's been dead for a century and a half? Is that possible? Is she sincere? In other words, does she really see Chopin the way that Delacroix or Liszt saw him in the 1830s? Or has Věra Foltýnova been lying and is she still lying to everyone about this? In that case, is she, if not the author, then at least an accomplice in a remarkably sophisticated hoax? I am going to answer these questions as accurately as I can, because obviously my conclusions will determine the angle of this peculiar documentary, the like of which I will probably never make again.

'"When you commissioned me to make this documentary, Filip, you made it clear to me that you thought my background as a scientific journalist meant I was the best person to tackle this kind of subject. The day you spoke to me about it, I didn't for an instant believe this story about meetings with Chopin, as you yourself can testify. And, in passing, I would like to thank you for providing me with the resources I needed to mount a surveillance operation on this musical fraud. I let Věra Foltýnova tell her side of the story; we filmed her at her apartment on many occasions. We accumulated a mass of interviews, during which she showed herself to be a cool, composed and reasonable woman who did not appear to be suffering from mythomania or any psychological problems. We slowly got to know this humble, apparently unambitious woman, who never ceased to intrigue me, while we awaited the results of the surveillance operation. Her letters were read, her telephone tapped, and we followed her wherever she went because we felt sure that, behind her, some brilliant con artist was hiding. We skimped on nothing. To begin with, our hopes were repeatedly dashed, but we persevered, convinced as we were that she would eventually make a mistake. For example, we filmed her one day when she claimed to be receiving dictation from Chopin. I can report that she played her role to perfection. It wasn't easy to find a chink in her armour.

'"So I set her a trap, in the course of our interviews. Has anyone here heard of Leslie Flint?"

'"The American porn king?" someone asked, sparking a wave of laughter around the table.

'"That's Larry," I corrected. "I'm talking about the medium Leslie Flint, who was later exposed as a charlatan... This person claimed that he had conversations with dead celebrities and that he recorded their voices. I got hold of the recording of the voice attributed to Chopin and we played it to Mrs Foltýnova, who fell straight into the trap. I asked her if she recognized that voice and she immediately replied that she did. 'That's the same voice I hear day after day,' she said. 'You've just played me the recording made by Flint, I assume?'

'"By crediting the works of that charlatan, she lost the first round. However, not all of my traps were so successful... Another day, when she said Chopin was in the room with us, I asked her to draw his portrait. We'd already noticed her talent for drawing; now it was up to her to prove that he was actually standing there. She hesitated at first, seeking a way out, but in the end she agreed.

'"I got a shock when she handed me the sheet of paper, let me tell you. The portrait she'd drawn *was* Chopin, and I found it hard to imagine that she could have made such a detailed sketch purely from memory. I was stunned. Angry with myself and with her too. Angry with everyone and everything.

'"I pinned all my hopes on the surveillance operation. On several occasions, I felt ready to give up. Never in my whole career had I felt so alone and so lost, not even when I was investigating complex legal cases or political scandals. I felt like I was caught in fog. And, when I talk about *giving up*, I don't mean abandoning the documentary, but being content to make a neutral documentary, something cautious and cold that wouldn't take a position on the truthfulness of what was being shown. A bit like a great chef microwaving fish fingers... I was within an inch of telling our viewers: 'Make of this what you will.' The detective tailed the impostor day after day and always came back empty-handed. All the different forms of surveillance turned up nothing. Our nets were empty. We felt pathetic, in the grip of something more powerful than us. This woman would regularly meet a friend in the Lucerna for a game of chess. I had the feeling that she was doing the same thing with us, and that she was always several steps ahead. Soon, she would checkmate us and the game would be over...

'"If that had been the case, though, I wouldn't be here speaking to you now. I'd have thrown in the towel, found another job... or at least a different subject. One day, during a conversation, a single word set me thinking. A word I hadn't heard before then."

'As soon as I said that, I felt a frisson of excitement around the oval table. I decided the time was right to make the most of their heightened attention. I knew I was beginning the most delicate part of my speech and that, soon after this, its fate would be sealed.

'"That word was a great help to me, indirectly. Because of that word, I was able to see Věra Foltýnova in a different light, to view the facts in a different way," I told them.

'I took a deep breath and my gaze swept the table. Then, without really addressing anyone in particular, I continued in a very deep, serious voice, a voice that didn't sound like me. I was like a medium in a trance, adopting the voice of the dead person with whom they're in contact.

'"Věra Foltýnova is not the author of a hoax. There is no hidden composer, no musical ghostwriter; this woman never intended to fool anyone. She is the most sincere person imaginable, the least ambitious person I've ever met. She has no ulterior motives. We have to admit the inadmissible: Věra Foltýnova has seen and continues to see Frédéric Chopin as clearly as I see all of you around this table."

'I could have just left them there,' I told Dana. 'In suspense. Without adding a single word. I'd come to tell them my conclusions, after all. Was there really any need to show them the reasoning behind it? Yes, on reflection, there was, if I was going to lead them where I wanted to lead them, because I could see the bewilderment and confusion in their eyes. Roman looked the most shocked of all, and I could understand that. Novák, too, was surprised, but he was smiling. He was waiting for me to go on – perhaps waiting for me to fall? As for the channel's president, he was frowning, perhaps intrigued, perhaps incredulous… I couldn't tell. But all of them were fascinated; they were hanging on my words. That was when I decided to tell them about the word that had set me thinking in the first place. I told them about my girlfriend, about her interest in orientalism and the strange spiritual resources of Tibetan lamas.

'"One day, when I was talking to her about Věra Foltýnova and her visions," I told them, "she said, half jokingly, that perhaps it was a tulpa in the form of Chopin. That word, which I'd never heard before, was like a slap in the face. As far as I understand, it is an emanation of the mind. The psyche of a person who has undergone years of training in certain forms of meditation can engender an entity, which then becomes more or less independent of its creator... And no, I don't believe for a second that the Chopin who dutifully visits Mrs Foltýnova is a tulpa, but it's strange how one word can suddenly change the trajectory of your thoughts. Like a billiard ball ricocheting off the cushion. Or like the golden beetle that flew against the window and reminded Jung's patient of her dream, for those who know that anecdote. It was on that day that, after so long going round in circles, I decided to broaden the scope of my investigations. From that instant, I stopped thinking only in terms of hoaxes, frauds and hidden ghostwriters. Perhaps I had to look elsewhere, at the deformities, anomalies and strange eccentricities of the human mind, whose depths remain mysterious. I began reading books I'd never opened before. I met neurologists, psychiatrists. Yes, it's astonishing how a single word opened my eyes. Some credible orientalists claim to have created that sort of entity and then seen it evolve. But of course Věra Foltýnova was no Buddhist! She didn't practise any form of meditation, unless you want to count old-fashioned Christian prayer. And – I say again – this was not a case of one of those entities that detaches itself from its creator, in certain very precise cases."

'I'm pretty sure, Dana, that while I was talking about wandering entities, some of them were thinking about Rabbi Loew's Golem, the clay creature that haunted the back streets of the Jewish quarter in the sixteenth century. But, unlike the legend of that terracotta Frankenstein, a tulpa is made not from matter but from the mind, and that was what I wanted to talk to them about: the human mind. This continent that we have only just begun to explore.

'"Science," I went on, "is a snapshot, at any given moment, of man's knowledge and ignorance. Until the end of the nineteenth century, the most enlightened minds represented the atom and its electrons as a star with its court of planets. Soon afterwards, quantum mechanics revealed this to be completely untrue. And yet, for a long time, it was the truth. What would a physicist of 1880 have thought if we'd told him that an electron was not always a point of matter, but a small wave in constant motion? And that, in a way, the universe was not composed of solid matter but of vibrations? He would have cried heresy. And, on the basis of what was known at the time, he would have been right. Back then, a human mind did not have the necessary knowledge to admit it, perhaps not even to imagine it."

'"What would that physicist from 1880 have said if we told him that, at every instant, billions of neutrinos were moving through his body, through his brain? What would he have said about those particles from the depths of the universe that pass through everything – concrete, the earth's core, living beings – at every instant? He would have responded that this was science fiction, not science. And yet, it's all true. Galileo! Even the great Galileo was tripped up by his own rationalism: he laughed when Kepler announced that tides were caused by the gravitational force of the moon. And Galileo was himself attacked for his work on heliocentrism and forced, during his trial, to deny his convictions, because in 1633 the Earth did not orbit the sun.

'"With our 1990s knowledge, we are in the same position. Our mind struggles to glimpse the discoveries to come, which will revolutionize our understanding of the world.

'"However, like Kepler with tides, like Galileo with heliocentrism, certain physicists are exploring beyond the limits of our current knowledge. You know Plato's allegory of the cave: men chained up inside it watch shadows on the wall – the shadows of people passing behind them, outside the cave's entrance; for these chained men, reality consists of those shadows and nothing else. But the shadows *are* alive. The men in the cave cannot grasp the idea that the shadows are merely the projection of a reality that they cannot see.

'"A number of scientists today believe that many of the phenomena we witness are perhaps merely shadows on the wall. Is it quantum physics that causes them to doubt the certainties on which our society is constructed? I am sure it plays a significant part. Who could have imagined that the ultra-materialist Soviet Union would take seriously phenomena such as telepathy or hypnosis? Experiments were conducted on thousands of subjects in the Fifties and Sixties, and the scientists even published their results. For example, Leonid Vasiliev, a student of one of Pavlov's partners, carried out some very interesting research on tele-hypnosis. And in the United States, NASA was studying the possibilities of telepathic communication.

'"So, you see, the opinions of great minds have changed radically in the last few decades. Fifteen years before receiving the Nobel Prize, Feynman created a disturbing theory: he believed that certain particles had the ability to move backwards in time, to move in both directions, towards the future and the past. Can you imagine? According to his theory, it would be possible for these particles to cross through the border of time in both directions, not only from the past to the future! Matter could embark on a return journey! Another Nobel winner, John Eccles, was interested in the idea of 'fields of influence' allowing two minds to communicate using only their thoughts. There are plenty of examples of rational minds believing that those shadows are not the full extent of our reality.

'"To conclude, I would also quote Wolfgang Pauli, the man who discovered neutrinos. Awarded the Nobel Prize for Physics in 1945, Pauli was very interested in questions of extrasensory perception, and his name is associated with that of Carl Gustav Jung, with whom he forged the notion of 'synchronicity'.

'"These are just a few of the most illustrious examples. Vasiliev, Pauli, Eccles, Kepler, Galileo, Feynman and others passed through science's Pillars of Hercules. We have no reason to feel ridiculous if we, too, are interested in the little-known capacities of the human mind. Need I remind you that for millennia, millions – no, billions – of people have blindly accepted the idea of an all-powerful god, without the slightest shred of evidence to support its existence? And why shouldn't we pay attention to things that science has not yet explained but that the greatest minds are investigating?

'"I've already told you about the wrong paths I went down during the making of this documentary: the idea that it was all a sophisticated hoax, with or without the involvement of a ghostwriter; the idea that a dead composer was visiting this world to finish the work he began while alive… And I have also told you of my conviction that Foltýnova really did see Chopin, which would explain why she was capable of drawing his portrait so well. Was she suffering from hallucinations? Was her subconscious playing tricks on her? I don't think so. My hypothesis is the only one that our knowledge cannot refute.

'"During the last few weeks, I've interviewed biologists, physicists and neurologists about the little-known capacities of the human mind. Some of you will probably find my conclusions provocative; others may judge them far-fetched. But they are based on what I was able to draw from the cutting-edge knowledge and intuitions of today's leading scientists. The dew of knowledge. In my opinion, Mrs Foltýnova appropriated Chopin: his personality, his talents, his emotions. This is not an act of theft in the traditional meaning of the word; more a case of impregnation. How? By accessing the world's deepest dimension. Each of us – in the same way that we are home to billions of moving neutrinos at every moment of our lives – is part of the collective memory. As a medium, Věra Foltýnova has a sensitivity for sensory experiences far beyond the average human's. She is more steeped than us common mortals in the tiny drops of that enormous cloud of floating consciousness, like the shelves of an infinite library surrounding us, where everything is recorded. I would say that she 'received' (or attracted?) Chopin's personality. She was able to connect to him because his consciousness and his memory endured, as everything does. Something in him was brought back to life by this woman who claims to have taken dictation of his compositions. She is subject to an illusion – her Chopin is not what she believes – but this illusion has nothing to do with hallucination. I don't know how else to say it; I have reached the limits of comprehensibility... I know she's sincere, and I have told you of my firm conviction. There is one thing, however, that I cannot explain: why, when she listened to Leslie Flint's recording, did she say she recognized Chopin's voice?

'"So my conclusion is that Věra Foltýnova is not an anomaly or a freak from a cabinet of curiosities; on the contrary, I see her as the vanguard of what humanity will perhaps become if, one day, we reach the end of our exploration of the brain and its possibilities – the possibilities opened by the field of telepathy – and the mysterious cloud of 'collective memory' that surrounds us. All we need is patience. A few generations from now, we will see more clearly, and perhaps everything will become perfectly comprehensible."

'The end of my speech – my invitation to wait a few generations – managed to loosen them up a little. I saw people smiling, looking less confused. But when I stopped speaking, the silence that followed was the most intense I've ever experienced. For a few seconds, everyone froze – their faces, their eyes, their hands – as if all fifteen of them wanted me to repeat what I'd just said to be sure that they'd heard me properly. There wasn't even any of the usual coughing or throat-clearing that you hear during silences at concerts. The silence lasted until Novák thanked me and asked me when the editing process would be complete.

'I didn't know what to do with myself. I felt suddenly freed of a heavy burden, but instantly a new anxiety took its place. I would have preferred looks of hate, whispered sarcastic remarks or open dispute to that silence, which was followed by conversations so ordinary that it felt like I'd never said anything at all.

'It was in that strange state of mind that I began editing the documentary later that day. Was it possible that all my research, my journey towards the outer edges of science and the known world could provoke nothing more than this bizarre ostracism? Perhaps I just had to be patient, to give them time to think it over. Or perhaps... The telephone rang then, bursting the bubble of my early-evening isolation as I was about to go home after three hours with the film editor. I had been expecting that call all afternoon, dreading it...

'Five minutes later, sitting behind his desk, Novák said: "So... how can I put this?" To my surprise, his tone wasn't cutting or arrogant. I'd been worried that he would say something so provocative that I'd fly off the handle, but he wasn't like that at all. He couldn't meet my eye, and I suspected that this was not a good sign. I didn't rescue him from his embarrassment; I let the silence grow thicker. I had been open with all of them about how I saw things, I had been as honest as I could, and at that moment I felt liberated. I had done everything I wanted to do, everything I believed I should do, and now, deep down, I didn't care if I'd burnt my bridges, if I'd fallen into his trap.

'How could he put it? Yes, that was the only unknown here, because beyond that I had little doubt about what he was about to tell me. I sensed that, up to a certain point, he would agree: edit the documentary, Ludvík, I'm sure you'll produce something excellent, as you always do – I could hear his paternalistic tone already – but, beyond a certain limit – how can I put this? – control yourself. Tread carefully. And I sensed that the borderline was marked by the very word that Zdeňka had pronounced. "We've given it a great deal of thought, Beran [the channel's president] and I," he was going to tell me in a murmur heavy with the implication of pros and cons weighed, hours of mature reflection, followed by an unequivocal decision. "It's an interesting story, an interesting theory, we like it, and we greatly appreciated your sincerity this morning, your passion," he would tell me in a few seconds. "I don't want you to think that we have a problem with you – not at all. We are big fans of your work. But… how can I put this?"

'I let him entangle himself in words, not for the pleasure of seeing him falter, but because I was being gradually overcome by a strange apathy, a hollow feeling. The words of a poet came to my mind: "I am a shelf of empty bottles." That was exactly how I felt; never before had I understood so fully that man is alone with his own defeat; deep down, his sincerity, his theories, his firm convictions are of no interest to anyone else.

'"The decision isn't mine, even if, it's true, I share his opinion; the decision comes from the very top, as you can imagine, and – even if I wanted to – I wouldn't be able to oppose it."

'I listened to the arguments of my Pontius Pilate. Or rather, to believe what he was saying, the arguments of a higher being. Instead of developing my conclusions, I was being asked to explain nothing, to stick to the simple facts. It would be a mistake to try to explain this phenomenon, he repeated; that's what I remember most clearly. "As for your theories... listen, do you really believe them? You always struck me as much more rational than that, Ludvík, in the past." (I preferred not to reply.) "Your theories, whatever their worth, which I am not contesting, cannot be heard by the general public, not today. It's probably too soon. Perhaps tomorrow. But we have to deal with the world as it is today, don't we? There's nothing to be done; that's just how things are." So, to sum up, he would prefer a smooth, neutral product that could be sold to foreign TV channels; above all, he wanted something accessible, something for everyone. Twenty-six minutes should suffice, he concluded.

'That was the verdict. My fifty-two minute documentary had been cut in half, because of my iconoclastic conclusions. I felt like a soldier who's just been demoted in front of his comrades.

'I left his office and sleepwalked downstairs. I knew I would have to walk through the editorial room if I wanted to reach the end of this day: the cold and darkness outside.

'I thought back to my initial fears, which I'd put down to paranoia: Novák, aware of my relationship with Zdeňka, was seeking vengeance by ordering me to make an impossible documentary. The truth was probably more prosaic: the theories I'd come up with were just not suitable for a mainstream TV channel. And apart from the drastic cut in length and the change of angle, apart from the feeling of humiliation, which would fade in time, I wouldn't face any other consequences. I just had to accept this failure and move on. As for that small Tibetan word – Zdeňka's little gift to me – well, perhaps that had been the poisoned chalice.

'On my way out, I bumped into Roman. He didn't look his usual cheerful self. In fact, he looked so gloomy that I stupidly thought that something terrible must have happened to him, something much worse than what I'd just suffered, like the death of his sick brother. How wrong I was, yet again! Dana, I'm going to have one last beer to help me finish my story. Have one with me, won't you? I promise we're close to the end now. I need to hammer one final nail in the coffin of that day, and then you'll know everything I wanted to say back then. Roman – whose optimism and simplicity had buoyed me up during all those weeks – spoke to me with cold fury. "We worked together all that time," he began. "I thought we were partners. After a while, I realized that wasn't true. All the time we spent interviewing her, you greeted her words with a sarcastic grimace, and then – without telling me anything, as if you were ashamed of having been so wrong – you do a load more interviews without even bloody informing me. So now, finally, you admit that she was sincere, even though it was completely obvious from the first interview – to everyone but you. And you wouldn't even listen to me when I tried to tell you…"

'So Roman executed me in a few short sentences, then turned on his heels and left before I had time to explain that, when I changed my mind, I was torn between indecision and hope, and I didn't want to talk to him until I felt closer to the truth.

'None of what we kept in the final edit was dishonest, Dana, but – after the documentary was shown – I didn't dare get back in touch with Věra Foltýnova. She didn't contact me either. Should I put her silence down to all her media duties, all the interviews she had to do, how busy she was? Or was it because she was disappointed by the lukewarm twenty-six minutes I'd produced, reviewed and corrected almost frame by frame by Novák, which had – and this was my only consolation – at least allowed me to make it clear that no hoax had been revealed, despite our surveillance operation?

'The show was broadcast. Time passed. Days, then weeks. Springtime returned. I got used to the idea that I'd never hear from Mrs Foltýnova.'

'So you never had any contact with her again?'

'Hang on, you'll see… She sent me an invitation to a concert performed by Peter Katin. She was there too and played several pieces, but, since she wasn't a great pianist, Katin played most of it. I could have gone to see her afterwards, but I didn't. From time to time, by chance, I would hear Věra on the radio. Success didn't seem to have changed her. She still sounded like a teenager, very modest, amused by how things had turned out…

'We had no direct contact for… probably more than a year. I assumed she'd been hurt, offended by my documentary, even though it had shown her in a good light. Was it because I mentioned the whole surveillance operation we subjected her to?

'Then one night, when I got home, I noticed that the light on my answer machine was flashing. I had a sort of premonition that it was her…'

XIX

'Listening to the message she'd left, I heard once again her jovial, composed voice. That woman's serenity never failed to surprise me. She apologized for not having thanked me for the "programme", laughing as she said she'd been carried away by her life as a "star". She'd call back later.

'I didn't give her time to do that. There was something slightly odd about the little pauses she left between her phrases; she didn't usually do that, and I felt an urge to call her back straight away. I sensed she had something to tell me that she couldn't say in the phone message. Or rather that she *had* said, between the lines. In those strange little moments of silence.

'I called her and we talked for a short while about the big media storm she'd been through and how she'd dealt with this sudden celebrity. She was as down to earth as ever, distancing herself from it all with her sense of humour and her sense of perspective. She didn't say a word about the documentary. I asked her if everything was all right now that the wave of success had receded and if she needed anything. She replied slowly that yes, everything was all right. Then I waited as she sank into silence.

'"There is something I'd like to talk to you about, Ludvík. Would you have time to come over for tea one day this week?"

'So here we were. *Something.* "Is it urgent?" I asked.

'"No, it's fine, there's no rush. But I think you might find it interesting."

'We met at her apartment the next afternoon. I must admit, I felt slightly nostalgic when I saw the flower-patterned wallpaper again, the drawings on the wall and all her little knick-knacks on the furniture. None of it had moved a millimetre in the past year, and the room was still filled with the same faint scent of lilac.

'"A few days ago, Chopin visited me. I see him less and less these days, but there he was. And this time, he wasn't alone... A man I'd never seen before stood next to him. Chopin introduced him to me: Viktor Ullmann... I knew the name of this Jewish composer – he's often mentioned, for example, when people talk about the Nazi atrocities – but I'd never seen a photograph of him. He was elegant, smiling. His had fine black hair, with a high forehead, a bit like an Asian man. He spoke to Chopin in German, and addressed me in Czech. He needed my help."

'"You'd never heard his music?"

'"I knew *Der Kaiser von Atlantis*, the opera that he wrote at the concentration camp, Theresienstadt. That's all. I went to Theresienstadt, a long time ago, to visit the Small Fortress, never imagining that anyone would have had the energy to write an opera there, when they were close to death every day... After a while, Chopin left us alone. I found it hard to maintain the contact and to hear clearly what Ullmann was saying to me. Was

I disturbed by the sounds of the city at that time of day, with its car noise and its church bells? Sometimes, with Chopin, when I wasn't feeling well, I would find it impossible to concentrate. He would quietly withdraw when that happened. I finally managed to understand that Ullmann was talking about his *Kaiser von Atlantis*, which had somehow escaped destruction. He hadn't had time to perfect it at Theresienstadt because he'd been sent to Auschwitz, where he was killed. He came to me because he wanted to dictate a few finishing touches… I did what he asked, despite the communication problems. In one place, he explained, the rhythm was marked by a minim followed by a crotchet, and he'd now decided that it would be better the other way around. How is it?"

'"Sorry?"

'"Your tea."

'"Oh. It's good. Very good."

'She smiled, realizing that I was impatient to hear the rest of what she had to say. "So, yes, he dictated a few modifications to me," she went on, "although I didn't have the score in front of me. In another passage, he wanted to replace a harpsichord with flute, violin and cello. I wrote that down too… After a while, as I was finding it harder and harder to receive Mr Ullmann, he disappeared. I didn't know what to do with all the notes I'd taken. Pass them on to Peter Katin, who knew lots of music publishers? Should I do it straight away? Ullmann hadn't given me any instructions. Were there other changes he wanted to make first? I wondered if he might try getting in touch with me again, since we'd had so many problems with the communication. Two weeks passed, though, and

I concluded that he wouldn't visit again. And then, three days ago, he reappeared."

'"Alone?"

'"Alone, yes. He was smiling, but he seemed more awkward than he had before. This time, I could hear him more clearly. To start with, he didn't ask me to do anything, he just talked about his life in Theresienstadt, where, strangely, he was given the freedom to compose and interpret his work. He was even allowed to rehearse *Der Kaiser*, which is an opera about death, but the SS realized that it was targeted at Hitler and they wouldn't let the performance go ahead.

'"In late summer 1944, Ullmann felt hopeful again. The Russians were moving closer, the Americans had landed in France... But that was when new trains started leaving for the north, to the extermination camp. Ullmann had composed about fifteen works in Theresienstadt, and when he realized that the noose was tightening, he tried to find a way to get them out of there. His friend, the philosopher Emil Utitz, the director of the camp's library, hid the scores for him. Ullmann pleaded with him to stay alive and take his music out of the camp because he felt sure that, wherever he was going, he wouldn't be coming back. Utitz was to keep the manuscripts and then return them to Ullmann if he survived – and, if he didn't, he was to hand them over to a writer called Hans Günther Adler, which is what he did.

'"Why did Ullmann tell me all that? When his story was over, he left a small silence and then said: 'The scores that Adler had have already been published and performed. But people think Utitz kept everything I gave him, and that's not true. At one point, he, too, was afraid that he'd be sent to Auschwitz and he gave some of the manuscripts to a friend. His hope was that, with my work divided between two people, at least some of it would have a chance of escaping the Nazis' clutches. But it is precisely the part of my work that he gave to this friend that has not yet resurfaced, and I would like it to be found.'

'"I asked him why Utitz hadn't searched for the missing part. 'Because his friend disappeared,' Ullmann explained. 'He was presumed dead, but in the confusion – when the camp was left in the hands of the Red Cross, then liberated by the Soviets – nobody could work out where he was, or even if he was still alive. He was a German-speaking Jew from Prague.'

'"According to Ullmann," Věra went on, "this man was in poor health and he'd died not long after Theresienstadt was liberated. His wife, who'd survived in hiding, emigrated to Switzerland. She remarried a few years later. The manuscripts would now be in the possession of her daughter, who lives in Zurich."

'Mrs Foltýnova didn't actually ask me for anything. But I was starting to know her quite well by now. She wouldn't have dared ask me openly. And yet, it was clear what she wanted me to do. She was normally so frank, but that day she couldn't meet my eye. My documentary had been broadcast long before, and she knew that I had moved on to other projects. She had no reason to turn to me at that moment. What was I, to her, that day? A confidant? A backup? I must admit, I was touched. It warmed my heart that she should think of me for this. Perhaps this was her way of thanking me for what I did before? She didn't get to the point, but she came close to it when she said, in a quiet voice: "I need to have a hip operation next month. The past year's been exhausting, with all this activity, all these tours. It's getting harder and harder for me to move around, so they're going to give me a hip replacement."

'So it was that I found myself, one fine morning, ringing the doorbell at a house near Zurich. But, Dana, I think I need another drink before I take you into the entrance hall of that cool, damp villa, and I'm going to be unfaithful to my beer: a glass of rum is what I need to help me recount this final episode.

'To be honest, Zurich scared me. You have to understand: as far as the Foltýnova affair was concerned, I'd categorized and labelled everything in my head, so I was afraid that a new blast of air would blow everything into disorder. I'd more or less satisfied the need for clarification that exists in all of us, and the explanation that I'd given to the TV channel seemed good enough to me. But something drew me to Zurich. The same little thrill of fear that the gambler feels when he raises the stakes, I suppose.

'I was in Zurich for two days and then I left. A detective observing me at that moment might barely have noticed any change. True, I was wearing different clothes and I was better shaved than I had been when I arrived; but I doubt whether he'd have spotted the way I kept checking, somewhat compulsively, that my suitcase was by my feet.

'The person whose villa I'd visited forty-eight hours earlier wasn't the kind to cause difficulties. I didn't have to give her many details; she was content to glance at my Czech press card and to hear how my investigation to track down lost manuscripts had led me to her address. Between you and me, Dana, I didn't really believe what I was saying. I was simply there to make sure I'd dotted all the i's on the Foltýnova story.

'The woman in the lakeside house was in her sixties and we conversed in a very stiff *Hochdeutsch*. When our conversation was over, she promised me she would "look". She seemed genuinely interested in what I'd told her. Perhaps she was bored by her life, and I represented a touch of the unexpected. Whatever the reason, I felt like I could leave the matter with her. She suggested I return the next afternoon; in the meantime, she would do some searching.

'Believe me, if you'd told me at that moment that two days later I'd be staring at my suitcase like my life depended on it, I'd have thought you were mad. And when, returning to Mrs Foltýnova's apartment, I handed her Ullmann's yellowed scores, I had the impression that those pages were my unconditional surrender.

'Dana, have you ever heard the story of the distant border that would move while the border guard was asleep? Whenever he woke, he would notice that the dotted line was no longer in exactly the same place it had been the night before. Sometimes it was further away, sometimes it was closer. Never by much, but enough that our man would carry his sentry box on his back, like a snail with its shell, and walk towards the new border. Time would pass – days, sometimes months – and then he would have to move again. The border had a will of its own. On the whole, though, it was gradually moving away from him. The territory that he was guarding was getting bigger.

'This is not a tale of ancient China. It's a story about the border between what we know and what remains unknown.

The guard is you and me. Sometimes, like him, when I wake I have the feeling that the land I saw the night before, dense with weeds and undergrowth, has suddenly been cleared, and the borderline has moved further back.

'But the strange thing about that border is that it doesn't move in the same way for all people. Why? Perhaps because some people are more willing than others to carry the sentry box on their back and move to a new position. That's the price they have to pay. It happened to me several times, with Mrs Foltýnova. I have a terrible backache, thanks to that old woman! What I believe to be the truth keeps shifting. In my own way, I feel like I've pushed that border back, and I'm pleased to be able to pass my sentry box on to you. It's your burden to carry, if that's what you want. Curious minds, like yours, like mine, spend their whole lives fascinated by that border. It's our *Desert of the Tartars*. There aren't that many of us, guarding the unknown, watching the border fluctuate before our eyes. During certain periods, it barely moves at all. I wonder if human beings will manage to push it back all the way before they die out.'

'We'll see.'

'If you want to be optimistic, you could believe that your great-great-grandchildren might witness the beginning of an explanation…'

'And then?'

'Then?'

'Věra.'

'I think I buried those manuscripts from Zurich in the deepest, darkest part of my memory, hoping never to think of them again. But it was like something radioactive. Insidious. Invisible.

Nagging and, ultimately, poisonous. I gave her those scores and I never saw her again. The only thing that brought me back to her was her funeral, ten years ago.

'Although I'd deliberately distanced myself from her, her death had a profound effect on me. I felt hollower than I'd ever felt in my life. A singular hollowness. Sometimes, in the months that followed, I would find myself hoping that she was going to materialize in front of me and start speaking, in her down-to-earth way. I wanted her to talk to me and I wanted to be the only one who could see her, as if, when she departed, she'd bequeathed to me the gift that she always claimed to have. But apparently I'm not gifted in that way. Not "receptive", as they say.

'Yes, it was only when she passed away that I realized the space she had taken up inside me, even though we never saw each other again after the Ullmann episode. I think, without knowing, she opened a door inside me, deep within, and a breath of air came through that doorway that prevented me from suffocating. Because I must have been suffocating, without really noticing.

'One day, I discovered that the apartment on Londýnská was for sale. I contacted the estate agent because I wanted to visit it. I didn't want to buy it. I just needed to see it one last time, if only for a few minutes. To find some closure. It was empty, of course. On the walls, you could see the pale rectangles where her framed drawings had been. I thought about that interview when I'd pressured her into drawing Chopin, who was invisible to me. Was it him I expected to see there, appearing just for me, while the estate agent reeled off his sales patter? I looked at each room, asking inane questions about them. Nothing remained. Even the persistent scent of lilac had disappeared… After a while, I found myself in the living room, looking out the window: behind the window of the Luník across the road, a man was smoking. From a distance, that man looked a bit like Pavel Černý, and I imagined him laughing at me, as if to say: your investigation's not got far, has it? I wondered where he was now, after all those years… So I told the estate agent the usual things you say when you're not interested in an apartment – "Give me your card, I need to think about it" – and of course he replied with the standard formula: "Don't wait too long, sir, there are other interested parties."

'Now, this is your case, Dana. Oh… one last thing before I leave you to it. Do you know where Věra is buried?'

'Beside her husband, I assume?'

'A logical assumption, but no. She's in Vyšehrad Cemetery. The funeral took place in St Peter and St Paul Cathedral, and you can imagine my reaction when, after the ceremony, the coffin was carried to the very place where Věra went to gather her thoughts that All Saints' Day, back in 1995. Another mystery that I'm passing on to you, along with my sentry box. Had she already reserved that spot, all those years ago? Was she paying her respects towards her future self? Did she believe that, having transcribed the posthumous works of a great composer, she should be buried in a cemetery full of illustrious names – Kubelík, Ančerl, Suk, Dvořák and others? God only knows… It's yet another secret that she took with her to the grave: her grave. There was something diabolical about that woman, despite the gentleness and calmness of her appearance. You can see why I felt the need to move on, afterwards. Until her death, she was a constant reminder to me that nobody can ever be certain of anything. In the cathedral, and then outside in the cemetery, I spent my time staring at the other mourners, particularly the ones whose faces were unknown to me. There were a lot of people. You should have seen them! I couldn't help thinking that, somewhere among that crowd, was the *deus ex machina* of the whole…'

'Oh, you still have doubts?'

'A small, nagging doubt, yes. After the funeral, I wanted to follow all those people. Back to their homes. Into their lives. Into their brains. To find out, at last, who profited from the crime. And what if there hadn't been just one impostor, but several? What if all those mourners had gone back home to compose mazurkas, scherzos, preludes? In France, during the Renaissance, there was a poet by the name of Louise Labé. Only now are scholars starting to seriously consider the possibility that she was a front for a collective of poets. Why? Who knows… Five centuries later, the truth finally rises to the surface. So, for Chopinova… well, let's just say we have time.'

XX

HE HAD FINISHED his account. The young woman nodded and smiled, as if deep in thought. She'd been affected by what he'd told her, he felt sure of that. He'd touched a nerve. Was it the alcohol that was making her appear so beautiful and attractive to him now? Or was it because nobody had ever listened to him for as long or as attentively as she had, with those fatal, hypnotizing eyes of hers.

Night was no longer master of its destiny. With the first glimmers of dawn, the darkness hid wherever it could. The river was no longer the sinister oil slick of the last few hours but a slate-coloured glacis moving past the theatres and concert halls. On the roof of the Rudolfinum, the composers' statues would soon have a front-row seat for the sunrise, amid the rattling and jangling of the tramway. Ludvík thought about the tragicomic beginning of a Jiří Weil novel, in which the Nazis, wishing to knock the statue of the Jew Mendelssohn off the top of the concert hall, mistakenly remove Wagner's instead. And what about Chopin? Was he watching from up there, too? Was he glancing down, amused, at the human comedy below? Bells and crosses, cupolas and domes… The most powerful memories of Ludvík's life were nestled between the towers of the old city. For him, these would always be radioactive zones, where he wouldn't set foot again for a long time: the streets, benches and cafés where he had loved life in Zdeňka's eyes. Between those points of pain were winding roads where he'd become a man, where he'd lost himself in the wonderful subtleties of hope and joy. And then there were places like Londýnská, the graves in Vyšehrad, all those streets down which he'd followed Věra Foltýnova. Yes, all of that, and when he remembered how old he was he couldn't believe it for an instant: it had all gone past in a flash.

'Shall we go?' whispered Dana, a few centimetres from him.

Thirty years ago, he thought, this woman would have made a perfect spy. That strange mixture of distance and complicity… She hadn't even had to ask him any questions. That, surely, was the best way of conducting an interrogation. He wondered if she would find out more than he had. Who knew? Perhaps only a woman's mind could have deciphered the mystery of Věra Foltýnova…

They stood up. Now he'd told her everything he knew, he felt like hugging her. In the cool dawn air, by the riverbank, he forgot about the quarter-century that separated him from her. She had probably realized from the outset of the night that with her face, her smile, her eyes, she would be able to extract all the secrets of his soul. All his thoughts about Věra Foltýnova. Under the influence of alcohol, Ludvík had begun to believe that he was about to win the admiration he deserved, recognition of his true worth. Hadn't he felt exactly the same way in 1995? Couldn't the barrier of time be raised every now and then for him? The alcohol had magicked away all his caution and, now that they were outside, he felt invincible despite his wobbly gait and his slurred speech. And, as she thanked him for his time and asked if she could get in touch again if necessary, he tried to put an arm around her shoulders. Freeing herself from his advances, she burst out laughing to defuse the tension and frowned at him as if telling off a naughty child. 'Now, Mr Slaný, we're not going to spoil this lovely evening.' Then she thanked him again and walked away.

Nobody had witnessed the scene. There were no smirking faces nearby. What an idiot, he sighed. He took a few swaying steps forward, then steadied himself on the railing at the top of the embankment. Suddenly overcome by nausea, he vomited a precipitate of beer and bitterness over the barrier. After that, he started to feel better, but now that the nausea was receding, the stupid thing that he'd done detached itself from him and he was able to see it in all its hideous clarity. He'd found yet another way to make a fool of himself. He wished he could rush after Dana and convince her to forget that, to remember only the long, eloquent speech he'd given. Often – a quirk of his profession – he would fantasize that life was just a long film shoot and that, when it was over, the dead were led into an editing room so that they could eliminate the weaker scenes and keep only the parts that showed them in their best light. He'd behaved with Dana as if he were the same age as her, and she'd fled from him, leaving behind a wreck of a man, filled with self-hate.

Gradually, the breeze brought him back to the sober reality of a chilly dawn. He heard the quiet sounds of this dead hour: the rush of the river below, engine noise fading, and – far in the distance – the howl of an ambulance. How long had he been leaning in this position, his guts wrung out? He gave himself a few more minutes there, focused on himself, eyes closed. After all, there was nobody around. Humanity was at low tide and, if not for the cold, he could have stayed motionless for a long time. How many more times was he going to humiliate himself like this? Never again, he swore, now that clearer thoughts were irrigating his brain. He'd handed over the keys to the Foltýnova affair, and now Dana must be far away, satisfied with her spoils, removing Ludvík Slaný from her memory like a deleted scene while answering all the texts she'd received from other men while he, the old fool, had thought he was creating some special form of intimacy between the two of them with his flood of words. In the end, one humiliation more or less didn't really matter – he'd suffered much worse before – but the bitterness he felt, this time, was more bitter somehow, perhaps because he feared that this humiliation would not be followed by any more victories, by any achievement that might erase the shameful memory. Well, that was a good thing: all he had to do was draw a line under this. To turn the page, as they say.

Just after this thought had crossed his mind, he heard a small cough – the kind of discreet cough whose only purpose, usually, is to let someone know that you are there. Ludvík took a deep breath, but kept his eyes closed. He hadn't heard her come back. Did she regret how casually she'd rejected him? A minute earlier, he hadn't dared hope for this kind of consolation, but now here it was... Unless she'd come back in a fit of anger, to excoriate him for his attitude. It was this fear that finally made him open his eyes.

It wasn't Dana. It was some night owl, Ludvík thought, probably a drunk like him, his outline slowly swimming into focus. He was half right: it *was* just some passer-by, but the man didn't look even slightly tipsy. There was something strange about the figure approaching him, however. The man was in his thirties, walking slowly in Ludvík's direction, indifferent to his presence, strolling along without any particular objective. A sleepwalker perhaps, or just one of those people who enjoy the meditative silence of early morning, when the world is readying itself to begin another day... The man was backlit by a streetlamp, but Ludvík had the impression that he was some sort of dandy, and – most forcibly of all – he had a sense of déjà-vu. But where could he have seen this man before? It would happen occasionally that he would greet someone whose face was vaguely familiar, and he would then spend the next few hours digging deep into his memory to find the person's identity, only to discover that it was just some bureaucrat he'd once spoken with in an office somewhere.

The man with the strange outfit had come alongside Ludvík and was about to pass him when their eyes met. To Ludvík Slaný, it was like an electric shock. The early-morning stroller continued on his way, but the moment that had just happened had the tessitura, all the characteristics, of a nightmare. He wanted to catch the man up and stop him, but his body wouldn't obey his commands.

It wasn't the alcohol or the nausea, because he felt suddenly sober now: that second of recognition had been like a bucket of cold water thrown at his face. He could only watch as the man moved away and turned at the corner of the street, apparently unfazed by their encounter: his hands were joined behind his back and his gait was so tranquil that Ludvík wouldn't have been surprised to hear him humming some melody that he'd composed long ago, before his death, or perhaps a new tune that had come to his mind in the silence of dawn, and that he would soon write down, after he'd returned from this visit to the land of the living.

Now that the man had disappeared, all that remained of his presence was a faint scent of lilac, quickly dispersed by the breeze.

ANY READER who wishes to know more about the life of Rosemary Brown can read the three books she published, from which I drew several elements:

Unfinished Symphonies: Voices from the Beyond (William Morrow, 1971)

Immortals at My Elbow (Bachman & Turner, 1974)

Look Beyond Today (Bantam Press, 1986)

I would like to thank Jean-François Zygel for patiently answering all my questions, and the Institut Français for the Stendhal Grant that allowed me to spend a long time in Prague in 2001.

ALSO AVAILABLE
IN THE WALTER PRESENTS LIBRARY

AVAILABLE AND COMING SOON FROM PUSHKIN PRESS